Other Books by Trilogy Davis

Arabella and the Tower of Magic Coming 5/1/23!

Odessa Book 2 Coming Soon!

When Life Gives You Pineapples Coming Soon!

ODESSA
AND THE
FIRST CONSTELLATION

Trilogy Davis

Trilogy Effect, LLC

TRILOGY EFFECT

This is a work of fiction. Names, characters, places, and incidents either are the product of the author's imagination or are used fictitiously. Any resemblance to actual persons, living or dead, events, or locales is entirely coincidental.

First paperback edition 2023

ISBN 979-8-9867960-0-0 (paperback)

www.trilogyeffect.net

Acknowledgments

Thanks to Erica, for bringing my characters to life.

Thanks to Calvin, for bringing my world to life.

Thanks to you, it took three years to finish this book, but I thank you for joining Odessa and I on our journey!

The Kingdom of Damasyr

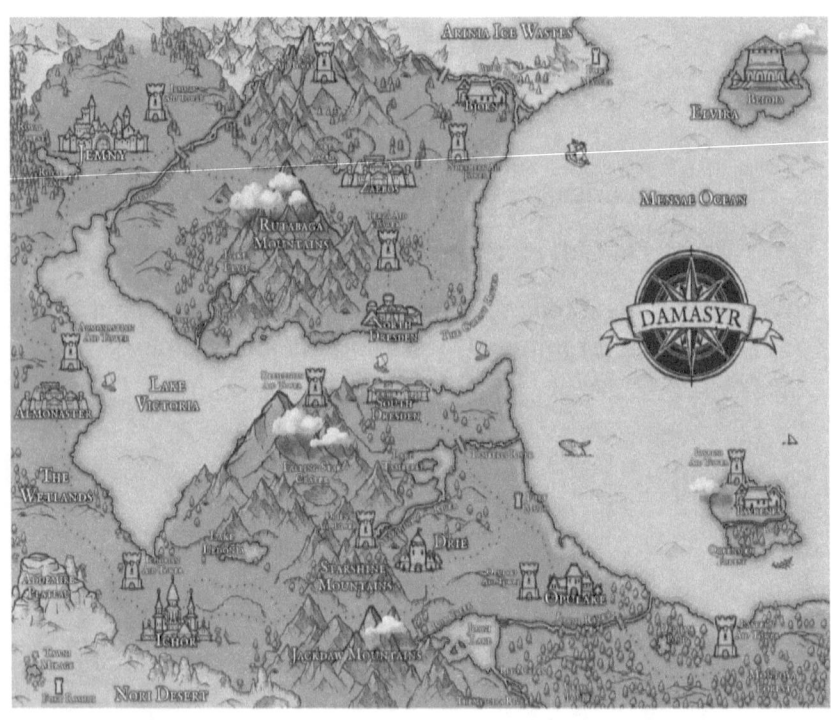

Table of Contents

Chapter ONE

odessa

Under my hand was the heat of both suns, burning and raging.

The house was quiet. The days when it had been filled with the sounds of a happy family had long passed and recently the house was more silent than ever before.

I poured boiling water into a cup and watched the dry tea leaves swirl. As the tea settled I sighed, grabbed the cup and a warm, damp cloth, and walked carefully back to Grimke's bedroom.

The room was dark and humid. Resting the tea on the side table, I sat on the edge of the bed and tapped the cloth on Grimke's clammy forehead. He coughed; his body rattling as the bed trembled.

The smell of peppermint from the tea filled the air and mingled with the miasma of sickness that emanated from my father's body.

Grimke continued coughing, but his eyes remained shut. His short blond hair hung in strands and stuck to his sweaty skin.

"Wake up," I whispered, wiping the sweat from his forehead.

He had gone to sleep three days ago and hadn't woken up since. The first day, I wasn't worried; Grimke worked hard and deserved a restful sleep for once, but as night came, he still hadn't woken up.

I had tried everything to wake him the first night, but Grimke remained unconscious. On the second day, I sent two pigeons to Opulake and the Eastern Aid Tower, requesting a doctor, but I had not heard anything back yet.

Opulake was the nearest settlement to Pavrenes. It was on the mainland on the eastern coast of Damasyri kingdom and west of my island home.

Pavrenes was my home, and it was a hamlet that sat on an unnamed island in the Mensae Ocean. It would take days for the pigeon to reach their destinations, and the time that it would take for a doctor to reach Pavrenes would be even longer, if they even had doctors there.

The one doctor we did have, Reyna, had been drafted to go to Jemny, the capital city of Damasyr, to collaborate with the doctors there on a cure, leaving the people of Pavrenes with only her son, Colden.

Odessa and the First Constellation

Colden was my boyfriend. He was short with long brown hair and large brown eyes. Our fathers were best friends and we had grown up together. He was always one of my favorite people, and after years of friendship, we became more.

Colden was the first person I turned to when Grimke fell ill. He had come the first night and checked Grimke's vitals.

"It's too soon to tell if it's the plague," he had concluded, closing his bag, and leading me out of Grimke's room.

I let out the breath I'd been holding in, as I watched him examine my father.

"We have one tonic left," I replied, walking with him to the kitchen.

He washed his hands, accepted a cup of peppermint tea, and sipped it slowly as he thought.

"No. Until we can confirm that it's the plague, let's wait another day."

Waiting another day had been harder than it sounded. I was anxious about the result, and I had been trying to keep it from Talicia, but she wasn't stupid.

She soon realized that something was wrong with Grimke and had been trying to diagnose him herself. Perhaps she spent too much time with Colden.

Getting the plague was almost a guaranteed death sentence. All the previous Pavrenis who had gotten it had

3

died and I worried that Grimke would meet the same fate.

If it turned out he did have the plague, he only had a week or so before he would pass away if the symptoms and progression of the sickness were consistent.

The symptoms were predictable. First came the cough with strained breathing, then came the fever, and that was followed by a coma. After a few days of sleeping, the infected stopped breathing completely.

Despite the plague's traceable progress, we didn't have anything available to combat it besides the tonics, and this was the last one.

"Didn't I tell you to give him space?"

I gasped, jumping off the chair and turning towards the door. I'd been so focused on Grimke and my thoughts; I hadn't heard Colden enter the room. He stood by the doorway, clutching the brown leather bag that held his medical supplies.

Unlike his half-brother, Tanner, who kept more to himself, Colden was boisterous. His skin had a permanent tan from our weekly adventures. When he was younger he did not tan but I liked it as it complemented his green eyes.

As Colden walked to the bedside and placed his leather bag on the chair, I stepped back and covertly tried to clear the sleep from my eyes. Caring for Talicia and worrying for Grimke had worn me out. I was exhausted.

But nothing got past Colden.

"You need rest, Odessa," he said, frowning at me. "Wait for me in the kitchen, and when I'm finished, I'll join you."

He gave me an awkward hug where he wrapped his arms around me without touching me before emptying his bag and turning back to Grimke.

I walked out of the room and towards the kitchen. I straightened a crooked sword on the weapon rack and grabbed the paintbrushes that had been left out before rinsing them in the sink.

While Colden conducted his examination, I gripped my tea and sat by the table. Just days ago, this kitchen had been bright with life and laughter. Now it was dark and empty.

I must've nodded off to sleep on the kitchen table because I felt my eyes flutter open at the sound of Grimke's door creaking open.

Moments later, Colden appeared at the kitchen doorway. I smiled up at him, and though he smiled back, I knew him well enough to see that it was fake.

"Odessa," he said, "If you touched him, you should wash immediately. We're still not sure how it spreads."

I nodded.

The plague had no official name, but it had been spreading throughout Damasyr for the last two years.

Despite the Queen's efforts, its spread had yet to be contained.

With Pavrenes' island's isolation, we had remained untainted until last month. Grimke had set up a quarantine zone for those who had exhibited symptoms. He had overseen the construction of the gate ahead of time and it now split our small settlement.

Once Pavrenis had begun getting sick we were prepared, and the sick were quarantined on the other side of the partition as a safety measure.

The quarantine gate's design was different from anything else built in our hamlet. Many of the buildings had been built generations ago and were now faded and old, but the gate was brand new and painted in a glossy coat of dark green.

As I passed him, I saw the crate that carried the supply of tonics we'd received from Jemny a year ago and sighed. It was empty.

The tonic was no cure, but it allegedly prolonged the infected's life and increased the chances of recovery. Now we were out of tonics, and no one had recovered.

I staggered down the hallway towards our bathroom, exhausted and weak in every way. Tears welled at the edge of my eyes as I listened to Grimke's raspy breathing.

Grimke was an older man at the age of sixty-two, but despite this, he was in great shape and always moved with a vibrant vitality. He had a particular diet and ran daily, but none of that had kept him safe. It seemed no one was immune to the plague that raged throughout the kingdom.

"Odessa?"

Sitting on the stairs with tears streaming down her face was Talicia, my younger sister. Talicia displayed her emotions to the world like the innocent kid she was. And right now, she was scared.

We were night and day, her dark blue eyes, strawberry blonde hair, and fair skin was a complete contrast to my hazel green eyes, black hair, and light brown skin.

Taking a deep breath, I feigned what I hoped was a reassuring smile, and walked toward her.

"Hey," I said, stopping at the bottom of the stairway. "Give me a moment to wash, and then you'll do the same so that I can try my best to comb that monstrosity on your head."

Despite her tears, she mustered a giggle and ran towards her bedroom. It was an inside joke of ours as no matter how often Talicia's strawberry blonde hair was combed, it always returned to its default messy status.

"We're gonna be all right," I said, as I followed her.

It was an attempt to convince myself just as much as her. Things would get better, even though at that moment, I couldn't see how.

o

Fun fact: It was Grimke who was the mayor of Pavrenes. He led the hamlet, held committees, and was always looking for more ways to increase Pavrenes's status.

Even though I had been only sixteen at the time, he had appointed me as his deputy mayor the previous year. This had never really meant much before, but if Grimke was out of action, technically I would officially be in charge of Pavrenes.

I wondered if anyone would object to me taking charge and if the Pavrenis would respect my authority. Did I have the right to take charge? I was still just a teenager after all.

The citizens respected Grimke and he respected them, but I would not be surprised if anyone chose to elect themselves as leader instead. What would I do if that happened?

Pavrenes was but a hamlet with about a hundred citizens, and I had heard that Jemny had over ten hundred thousand citizens.

I could not imagine overseeing that many people. Despite its smaller size, the thought of being in charge of Pavrenes now filled my stomach with butterflies.

After washing Talicia's hair and giving her something to eat, I walked through the front door of our home and into the rays of the suns.

It was a sunny day, as most days were, but it was cold today. There was a strong breeze that persisted. I thought it would be perfect for sailing, if not for the storm clouds congregating in the distance.

A crowd had gathered in our yard. News of Grimke's sickness seemed to spread faster than the plague itself. Grimke had only missed a few days of work but that alone was enough to breed uncertainty in our hamlet.

A few of them had gathered in our yard last night, but with no news, they quickly dispersed. Today, however, it seemed like most of the remaining Pavrenis were in front of my home.

The talking and whispers died down and the atmosphere was as grim as our garden. It had died years ago despite my best efforts, although Talicia insisted it was making a comeback due to her efforts.

Colden's father, Jacob, and his brother, Tanner, were there, as well as the other villagers of Pavrenes. Jacob locked eyes with me and gave me a slight nod, which I returned nervously.

Jacob had always been there for me and besides Grimke and Talicia, he and Colden were my favorite people in the world.

"Well, are you going to say something?" piped Chelsea, the innkeeper. "I've got customers waiting."

Some of the villagers behind her rolled their eyes.

This was untrue. We'd not had any visitors in months, although our little island wasn't exactly a tourist spot to begin with. The closest thing to a tourist attraction we've ever had was the Queenslen Forest and Chelsea's inn was borderline closed.

The door behind me swung open and Colden came out. He stopped next to me and straightened his back, in a vain attempt to appear taller. I had towered over Colden since we were kids, and although he was catching up to me fast, he hadn't bested me yet.

"He definitely has the plague," Colden said, resting his hand on my shoulder.

A wave of nausea swept over me, as I struggled to keep myself composed. Colden turned to the crowd that had inched closer and addressed them.

"Everything's going to be all right," he said.

Wasn't that the same thing I just said to Talicia? Was he lying too?

I turned back to our house and glanced at Grimke's window, knowing that he was laying there, burning to a crisp. Two bright blue eyes peered back at me from the upstairs window, above his room. I needed to be strong for her.

Turning back to the crowd that had gotten bigger with Colden's announcement, I took a deep breath and suppressed my fear.

"The mayor appears to have the plague, so we need to transport him to the quarantine zone."

The crowd gasped and the whispers grew louder, as Colden gestured for his brother and Jacob to follow him back into the house. I didn't get to say goodbye before I'd had to address the citizens, and now, I wouldn't have the chance.

"What's going to happen now?"

"If Grimke can fall victim to the plague, we'll be next."

"At this rate, I'll have no customers for my inn!"

"All right," I said, loudly, as the talking died down. "We're completely out of the tonics we received from Jemny. Does anyone have any?"

Silence.

Grimke had been in the midst of getting help from Lord Laurens who was the Lord of Opulake to invest in the town, but the plague took over, and then things had gone downhill since then.

Grimke had fallen sick before a grant could be issued. Although I had lit the Pavreni Aid Tower, the Eastern Aid Tower remained unlit on the shore, and no one had come to help or investigate.

"Very well, I-"

The door swung open. Jacob and Tanner walked out of the house, carrying Grimke to the quarantine housing, with Colden following closely behind. About forty percent of Pavrenes resided there now. Tanner's mother, Ramona, was one of the many Pavrenes who rested in the quarantine area.

I felt the responsibility of my task weighing heavy on my shoulders. I'd had training for this, but training was different from action.

Goodbye for now, Father. I'll fix this, I promise.

"What now?" Chelsea asked.

"I'm going to journey to the Eastern Aid Tower, if not Opulake to ask Lord Laurens for more support for Pavrenes. It seems he hasn't received our pigeons. I'll be taking Talicia, and Jacob will take charge in my absence. It's about three days of travel total, so I will, with good luck, be back in seven, maybe eight days. If I must I will sail to Opulake but that is the worst-case scenario, I'm going to the Eastern Aid Tower first."

I had never left the island and I felt bad about leaving hours after taking charge, but Grimke was sick, so there was no time to wait any longer for a response by pigeon.

Tanner and Colden rejoined the crowd as those assembled began to disperse, but their father, Jacob had not returned with them.

"Hey," I said, beckoning him closer. "If you see Jacob, let him know that I'll meet him at your house after I've packed some things. Oh, and make sure to wash well."

Tanner nodded and left, while Colden made his way to my side.

"I guess I'll see you in eight days?"

"What do you mean?" he asked, an expression of confusion clear on his face. "You've never even been to Opulake, plus you can't swim. I'm definitely coming with you."

"You're the closest thing to a doctor we have. I need you to stay in Pavrenes and help where you can."

"Odessa-"

I touched his cheek and shook my head.

"I'll see you in eight days, nine at the latest. I promise you, Colden," I said.

The words slipped out my mouth like an unrestrained river even when I knew I should not have allowed my tongue to make promises so easily.

"Fine." He sighed, as he pulled me into a hug. "Good luck and safe travels."

He kissed my cheek, and at that moment, I closed my eyes and ignored the world around me. I felt warm and safe. In my heart, I wish he could accompany me.

"Thanks, Colden."

"I love you," he said, running his finger along my cheek.

"I know," I said, smiling at him.

With one last kiss on my cheek, he walked off toward his home.

Before I could turn around and into my home, the wind shifted, and the scent of oranges entered the air. I turned around and saw Momma Mahalia on my porch with her leather bag of bones.

Momma Mahalia was called that because she had a daughter who was also named Mahalia and we did that to distinguish between them.

The unique thing about Momma Mahalia was that she sometimes did fortune telling. I wasn't completely sure how it worked, but she rolled a twenty-sided dice and gave answers based on the results.

Her husband Marcellus had vanished at sea years ago and I'd heard that someone had heard her pleading for him not to leave, and that if he did, he would not return.

Marcellus had left and he had indeed not returned, and because of that, Pavrenis did not sail east of Pavrenes anymore.

The ocean stretched farther east than our maps charted, and Marcellus was an explorer. He had sailed out many times before and had always returned safely.

"Want me to read your fortune for your journey?" Momma Mahalia questioned. Her eyes glowed a brownish-red hue and her long red hair flew in an unrestrained manner with the wind.

The Mahalias and Talicia were the only ones on the island with red hair, although Talicia's hair was a lighter red.

I considered the luck seer's offer. I had never done it before, although I had wanted to. Grimke had the opinion that the future could not be predicted, and I agreed, but if it gave a positive response, I would feel better about my chances of success.

I thought about how a negative result might affect my mindset and decided against it.

"Thanks, Momma Mahalia," I said with a smile. "Maybe next time."

Momma Mahalia smiled, but her smile was tinged with sadness.

"There won't be a next time, honey," she replied.

"Are you okay? You're not sick, are you?"

"No, just old," she said with a chuckle. "It seems I am near the end of my life."

"Aw, don't say that, Momma Mahalia," I said sadly. "I'm going to get the cure and come back as soon as I can."

"I know you will," she said with a smile.

With that, she got up and walked down the road toward her home. Halfway down the road, Mahalia the Second appeared at her side and hugged her tightly.

The scene made me miss my own mother. With a sigh, I turned and faced the door of my home. I took a deep breath before entering.

Back in the house, Grimke's cough had been replaced with Talicia's whimpers, and there was nothing I could say to comfort her. Nothing but lies and false promises.

When the plague first arrived on our shores, I pleaded with Grimke to stay away from the sick, but he insisted that as the Mayor, it was his responsibility to make sure every villager was taken care of. Now it was mine.

Grabbing the worn leather bag hanging by the door, I gathered clothes for myself and Talicia, as well as rope, rations, my deputy mayor's paperwork, and the sword Grimke had gifted me.

It was a special sword made of black metal with a black hilt. It was one of a kind and I was convinced that Grimke had once been a knight of some sort, but he often denied it.

Back in the front yard, the crowd had now dissipated completely. A part of me hoped that Colden was still standing there, ready to insist that he join me. This time, I would've said yes.

The suns were high in the sky now as I made my way to the stables. As I approached the last stall, my horse, Scout, neighed happily at me. His deep brown fur shone in the light of Zaniah, the elder sun, and Astria, the younger sun. I ran my hand through Scout's blond mane, and he neighed.

"Sorry, boy, business again," I said somberly. How I longed for the days when Scout and I used to roam the island together just for joy of it.

Scout dropped his head and remained still as I strapped on his saddle and attached my bag. Once that was completed, I walked to the basket of apples and retrieved one.

Scout neighed as he devoured the apple. He then nuzzled my shoulder gently, requesting another. I glanced at the fruit bucket, but it was empty.

"Sorry, boy, that's it."

Grabbing his reins, I walked him out of the stables and to my front yard. Once he was secured to the hitching post, I brushed his mane and thought about our route.

We'd need to pass through the Queenslen Forest, and then it was a straight sail to the Eastern Aid Tower. But if we ended up needing to go to Opulake, that would be a much longer distance. We'd reach the beach and spend most of the journey in the Montoya Forest.

With a sigh, I turned and faced the door of my home. It was time to get Talicia.

As I swung the door open, to my surprise, Talicia was sitting on the stairs fully dressed in her riding gear, with her knapsack strapped on her back.

She was ready and I didn't have to say anything. I was proud of her and glad that I decided to bring her along. She was only twelve, but sometimes she acted so much more mature.

She stood up quickly, with her head high, and looked me in the eyes. There were no signs of tears or fear. She locked eyes with me and said confidently:

"Let's go save Dad."

17

Chapter TWO

estonia

Before we could depart for the southwestern coast of the island, I wanted to speak with Jacob and get his advice. Jacob spent most of his time at the butcher shop, but after everything that happened today, I knew he'd be home with his sons.

"Wait here," I said to Talicia as I secured Scout on the hitching post outside Jacob's home.

I knocked on the door and waited patiently as the sound of shuffling footsteps got closer.

Jacob's home was smaller than my own but much fuller with life and charm. The sitting room was filled with potted plants and quirky art, while their kitchen was bright and smelled of coconut bread.

You wouldn't think a man like Jacob could cook but his loaves of bread were splendid. Since the plague had hit the kingdom, it had been harder for him to get the ingredients he needed, and the treat of bread was much rarer.

Their thriving plants were a great contrast to my garden which looked like a flower's graveyard. Jacob's counters were occupied with shrubs and filled with daisies.

The door opened and Jacob peered through.

"Odessa," he called, stepping aside, and holding the door open.

"Jacob," I replied as I entered his home.

Colden was nowhere in sight. Masking my disappointment, I followed Jacob to the kitchen. He walked to the counter and started cutting out parts of the cow lying on it, while he baked some bread and had a tea kettle warming up on the stovetop.

"I'm going first to the Eastern Aid Tower, and if that doesn't work, going to Opulake is my plan B."

"Plan B is dangerous for someone who's never left Pavrenes."

"I'm the mayor now, which means I have no choice. When I leave, you'll be in charge."

Jacob grunted but said no more.

Like his son Tanner, Jacob rarely spoke, yet he was the one that Grimke trusted the most. He was smarter than most gave him credit for, and he'd spent his entire life on this island. If anyone could lead Pavrenes, it was Jacob, and although both his wives were gone, he still had Colden and Tanner at his side.

And right now, we had no choice, we needed the plague tonics.

He washed his hands and sliced some of the bread, wrapping each piece individually. He also stole some of Colden's favorite cookies and added them along with the bread in a small package.

"Thanks, Jacob," I said, smiling up at him.

With the rush of everything, I'd forgotten to pack food, which now seemed silly, in hindsight.

He gave me an awkward pat on the back, which was as close to affection as Jacob could muster.

After a quick goodbye, I left Jacob in the kitchen and let myself out. Once outside, I mounted Scout and helped Talicia do the same.

I felt slightly better but knew I would feel much better once we were on the road. I enjoyed horseback riding, and it was very relaxing for me.

"Ready?" I asked as I grabbed Scout's reigns.

She wrapped her arms around my waist.

"Ready."

And with a gentle tap of my foot, we were off.

o

To get to the Pavrenes Aid Tower, we first needed to pass through the Queenslen Forest. Over the years there had been many rumors and mysteries surrounding the Queenslen Forest, and as each year passed, the stories got scarier.

In school, Charlesetta swore that she had seen several pairs of glowing red eyes staring back at her one night when she'd gotten up and looked out the window.

While our friends whispered and gasped at her story, Colden and I made a vow to investigate the forest and uncover its mystery.

That was three years ago, and although we didn't discover any headless horses or strange old ladies, we did stumble upon a couple of lazy snakes and creepy-shaped trees that looked like giant wooden people.

Today the forest was quiet.

We rode in the darkness, enjoying the ride and listening to the sounds of Scout's gentle trot. Specks of orange light filtered through the trees as we neared the forest's exit. The suns were setting, and we needed to reach the aid tower before nightfall.

The air became chilly, and Scout's trot quickened. In the distance, I heard the whooping of a monkey as we broke out of the Queenslen Forest and into the neighboring fields.

Although the island had no roads, Grimke taught me every path and where each one led to. I guided Scout onto the path alongside the Resyr River and we arrived at the Pavreni Aid Tower before the darkness set in.

21

After securing Scout, I opened the aid tower door and helped Talicia settle in. We'd stay here for the night. In Pavrenes, the nights were short, so it wasn't long before Zaniah peeked at the horizon.

While the aid tower was still dark, I tiptoed around the room, gathered our things, and set out breakfast.

Once the sunlight filled the room, I nudged Talicia awake and handed her a piece of Jacob's bread. She took it and nibbled on it slowly, but it seemed neither of us had much of an appetite.

"Are you scared of the water?" she asked, putting the bread down.

"No," I said quickly. "Are you?"

She shrugged, but I saw the hesitation in her eyes.

"Nothing's going to happen," I said, leaning in and scuffing her hair.

She rolled her eyes at me.

"Odessa, you can't swim."

"That's what the boat's for," I said, and that got a smile out of her. She finished her bread, and we packed up our supplies.

We left the Pavrenes Aid Tower soon after and made our way to the docks. The Pavrenis had constructed three boats, and each floated alongside the small dock.

The smallest one, the *Estonia*, was the one we'd be sailing. It had a bright red hull, with pristine white sails. It was the only Pavreni boat built with one mast.

Grimke taught me everything he knew about boats. On my thirteenth birthday, I sailed for the first time, and by the time I was fifteen, I was steering the boat as we made loops around the island. This would be my first time sailing without him.

I helped Talicia off Scout and led her toward the dock. We made our way down the ladder on the side of the *Estonia*. The boat bobbled with the gentle waves. The worst part of sailing was always the first few minutes I stood on the boat. My legs always felt like jelly.

"You okay?"

Talicia had turned a delicate shade of green. I moved closer and grabbed her hand as she closed her eyes and held her breath.

"Breathe," I instructed. "If you're feeling seasick, lay down and after a bit, you'll feel better."

Leaving her laying down, I took our supplies and stowed them below the deck, before climbing back onto the ladder and returning to Scout who was happily nibbling on the blades of grass nearby.

"Good boy," I whispered, as he nibbled on the stale crackers I found below the deck of the *Estonia*. "Okay, it's time to go home, boy."

He nuzzled my cheek, before trotting on the path that led to Pavrenes. I stared at him until he vanished into the Queenslen Forest.

"You look better," I remarked, as I returned to the *Estonia* and checked on Talicia.

"I feel better."

"Great! Ready to help me angle the sails and raise the anchor?"

"You think?" she asked sarcastically, as she hopped up and followed me to the right side of the boat.

I bent down and touched the water with my hand. It was freezing, but there wasn't any ice in the ocean. This was a good sign. Grabbing the ropes, I showed her which one controlled the angle of the sails, and which one controlled the length.

We angled the sails and raised the anchor, which was long and tedious. At that moment, I missed Grimke's immense strength. Once the anchor was secured, we dropped the sails and watched as the wind caught them and filled them with life.

Even though it was a freezing winter day, the sea was calm and the winds gentle. This meant we'd arrive on the coast by the end of the day.

Because of our two suns, Astria and Zaniah, we had long days and short nights, with Ithil, our purple moon only rising and hanging in our sky very briefly.

I took control of the helm and angled it towards the Eastern Aid Tower. Once all the ropes were tight and the equipment was secured, I walked over to Talicia who was sitting at the side of the boat and staring out at the water.

"Hey," I said, sitting down next to her. "Would you like to hold the wheel?"

"Really?" she squealed, ignoring the strawberry blonde curls that whipped her face.

I smiled and led her to the helm. Once she was standing before the wheel, I cupped her hands in my own and placed them on the pegs of the wheel.

"This here is the compass, but we don't really need it, we just need to sail straight for that tower there," I said, as I gestured towards the Eastern Aid Tower on the coast of the Damasyri mainland.

We were in between the island and the mainland. The sky was clear, the water still calm, and there were no protruding rocks in the water.

I glanced at the sky and decided to climb the crow's nest and enjoy the view. It was my favorite spot when Grimke took us sailing. Standing there made me feel so close to Ithil.

"You've got this," I said, giving her hands a gentle squeeze before releasing them. "I'll be on the crow's nest, call out if you need me and I'll hear you."

Talicia gave me a nervous nod before focusing once more on the coast. It was her first time steering a boat, but the Eastern Aid Tower was right there, and I'd already aimed us in the right direction. All she had to do was keep us straight for the day and we would be fine. I would check up on her in a few hours.

I made it into the crow's nest and the view was just as beautiful as I remembered. Ithil was early in its ascent, but its violet light shone on me. I had always felt attracted to the purple moon.

But it was daytime, and Astria and Zaniah levitated in the sky. I would have liked to sail the previous night, but it was Talicia's first time sailing and I wanted to be as safe as we could on this journey.

I sat on the stool in the crow's nest and gazed out at the dark blue waves. The ocean was beautiful too, but it was a different beauty from Ithil. The ocean had a cold beauty and a forbidden love to it.

I couldn't swim, which made the mystery of the ocean grimmer and foreboding. How deep did it go? What was hiding in the ocean's depths? I closed my eyes and listened to the waves.

My stomach grumbled. We hadn't eaten since breakfast, and even that meal was pitiful. I was never the best cook, but Grimke was amazing, and his breakfasts were one of my favorites.

I thought back to a time when Grimke, baby Talicia, and my mother spent the morning seated around our now abandoned dining room table. The smell of lavender filled the room from the bouquet sitting at the center of the table. Lavender was my mother's favorite.

I had staggered towards the table, with a plate overflowing with chopped potatoes and a tall stack of pancakes.

At the breakfast table, we'd usually talk and laugh as a family, but this time my parents kept their conversation to themselves, and their words were short, quick, and low.

As they spoke in hushed tones, I fed Talicia some scrambled eggs from Grimke's plate. While Talicia smeared the egg around her mouth, Grimke pushed back his chair and left the room in a huff. I looked at him and then at my mother who was still sitting, with her head down.

"Odessa?"

Why did Mom look so sad?

"Mom," I called, ignoring Talicia's nudge for more eggs.

"Odessa."

Why did Grimke storm out? He never got angry in front of us. He rarely showed much of any emotion.

"Odessa!"

My eyes burst open. The younger sun, Astria, was already dropping on the horizon, and speckles of orange streaked the dark blue sky.

How long was I out? I wondered. Had we reached the shore? I stood up and looked around. We were still in the water, but the *Estonia* wasn't moving as quickly as it

27

had been. My eyes found Talicia, who was frozen in fear, pointing at the ocean.

Spinning around, I noticed the large ship parallel to ours. It was much bigger than the *Estonia* and constructed of dark wood and black sails that were speckled with connected red dots.

Two harpoons were wedged into the side of our boat that linked us to the larger ship. Four figures were hurrying from the deck of the dark ship towards ours. They were armed with weapons and torches.

Pirates!

I needed to protect Talicia.

Tearing the bottom of my shirt, I wrapped the strips around my hand and grabbed the nearest rope. I stepped back and then ran forward, swinging in the air, under the purple glow of Ithil.

Letting go, I fell onto the deck next to Talicia, hitting my head on the floor. I ignored the jolt of pain and staggered towards her. She was gripping the helm tightly, as tears rolled down her cheeks.

The Damsyri mainland was close by, if we could remove the harpoons, we could try to outrace them. The Eastern Aid Tower was usually manned by soldiers, Mystio, or Rangers. If we got there, we would be protected.

"Talicia," I cried, studying the harpoons. It would be impossible to remove with so little time, and water was trickling in from the holes the harpoons had created. "We need to cut the cords, now!"

While I watched the pirates grabbing onto the rope of the harpoon, Talicia appeared by my side with a small dagger.

My sword!

I pulled my sword from its sheath and aimed it at the rope. Although the rope was thick, my blade cut through it with ease.

The pirate howled as he was plunged into the ocean's raging waves with a *splash.*

I ran over to Talicia who was struggling to cut the other harpoon. Pushing her aside, I slashed the rope.

Splash! Splash!

"Repair the ship," I instructed, running to the side of the deck. While Talicia grabbed a couple of planks from below the deck, I angled the sails and quickly brought our boat to life once again.

"Odessa!"

One of the pirates was climbing onto our boat. Talicia smacked him with the wooden plank, but he still scrambled aboard, unaffected by her attack.

"Back up," I told her.

We watched in horror as another pirate climbed onto the deck. The first one dropped our anchor and the *Estonia* lurched to a halt.

As the man staggered towards us, I swung my sword at him. In one quick motion, he pulled out a sword, twisted his blade around my wrist, and I was forced to let go of my sword and it fell into the water that had leaked onto the deck.

"Odessa."

Talicia pushed her dagger into my hand. A gleaming "A" was on the red gem at the end of the hilt. I had never seen a weapon like it before but there was no time to study it further.

As the other pirate neared us, I realized that it was a woman. She was tall and slender with long black hair and pale white skin. Compared to the other grubby pirates, she was a giant.

Both the pirates wore all black with a red symbol of pointed dots connected by lines that formed some kind of winged animal.

"Careful now," she sneered in a low, cool voice, as her eyes dropped to the dagger in my hand. She was amused. To her, this was a game. She was the crouched cat, and I was the cowering mouse.

She lit the lamp that she was carrying and held it high in the air so she could see me better.

"Listen, lady," I said, but my words wavered, and my head was beginning to spin. "I don't have anything to spare, I have a town full of people to take care of. I'm on my way to the mainland for plague tonics. Please let me pass, people are dying as we speak, people I care about."

She shrugged, unaffected.

"Times are hard indeed, yet we simply require everything you have. Everyone has a sob story, darling. You won't find anything on the mainland, I'm afraid. This boat is now ours. So, if you don't want the girl to be hurt, you'll give us everything, including that nice little sword. So be a good girl, slide it over, and don't do anything silly now."

I glanced down at my sword, gleaming in the water. It was my only inheritance and my most prized possession. I glared at the woman before me. They'd have to fight me if they wanted this sword. These foul and despicable thieves deserved nothing.

I lifted the dagger, anger vibrating through my body. The first pirate staggered forward.

"Ah, this one's a fighter, Lieutenant Captain." He cackled, looking up at the woman.

"Yes," she replied, watching me closely as her underling closed in. "Jesuit would approve."

"Stop," I growled as the light of Ithil leaked through the clouds.

She laughed, unaffected by words.

"There's two of us and many more on the way," she said, gesturing at their ship.

The other pirates were standing on deck, waiting for the signal from their leader to climb the ropes.

"You're unskilled and outnumbered. It's best if you give up," she continued. "I can take you to my leader, Jesuit. He'd like you, so young and full of fire. You'd make a great addition to the First Constellation," she said with a honey sweet voice.

At her words, I realized that the symbol was a constellation of some sort. I had never seen an animal as large as the symbol. It looked similar to the body structure of a bird, but it was hard to tell.

"Never," I shouted. "I'd faster die than become a pirate."

"Maybe." She shrugged. "But with you gone, what shall we do about your sister? We'd make use of her."

As Ithil's light washed over me, I felt my anger rising. No one was going to hurt my sister. No one was going to stop me from reaching the Eastern Aid Tower. No one was going to stop me from saving my people.

My ears started ringing and my body trembled as the pressure built within me, threatening to burst.

For the first time since they arrived, the pirates looked anxious.

"Don't-" the man began.

But it was too late.

"I told you to stop. Now!"

The pressure within me was released, and the man fell back onto the deck with a loud splash. He lost his grip on his sword and it sunk below the water.

"Your eyes," croaked the woman, stepping back.

I turned my gaze to her.

"Drop," I said, and moments later her eyes rolled up and she fell into the water that had accumulated on the deck.

My eyes?

I glanced at my reflection in the water and gasped. My face was streaked with filth and my eyes were no longer hazel, and instead, they were light purple.

The pressure within me slowly faded, and as it did, my eyes returned to their hazel hues. Suddenly, reality dawned. The water was at my shins now and the roars could be heard from the other ship.

Another harpoon pierced our boat.

"Talicia," I called, turning towards her, "I need your help to cut the harpoon."

She nodded and grabbed my sword from the water.

"Odessa, here."

She passed it to me, but I couldn't hold on to it. I felt tired. More tired than I had ever felt before. I tried cutting the rope of the harpoon, but unlike the previous two, this one was harder to cut. My legs felt like jelly and my arms were as stiff as clay.

I felt myself falling back and plunging into the dark water. As the water slowly cloaked me, I heard Talicia cry out above the water's surface but I was unable to move and I sank into an endless ocean.

Chapter THREE

arabella

"So, you don't ever want to leave the island?"

Colden and I were on another one of our adventures, but this time, instead of horseback riding through the island or exploring the Queenslen Forest, we decided to take a walk through the village.

It was the first day of the Pavreni Moon Festival and the whole hamlet was on holiday for the most part so that that everyone could attend. Colden and I had gone every year together and that would change no time soon.

I loved interacting with the various merchants who sold overpriced trinkets and food from distant places. I looked forward to night, as once the suns set and Ithil took reign of the sky, fireworks would be let loose to light up the sky with colors of white and violet.

"For what?" he asked, with a smile. "Everything I need is here. My father, my mothers, my brother, you."

"Really?" I sighed sarcastically, shaking my head. "I'm last on the list."

He laughed, pushing me forward. I spun around to face him and continued walking backward. Today was a particularly hot summer's day, and right now it felt as though both suns were pointing directly at us.

"I mean, we've been here our whole lives; wouldn't you like to go on an adventure? We have all of Damasyr to explore."

He sighed, grabbing my hand, and pulling me into him, as he kissed me softly.

"Well, Odessa, I'd followed you anywhere, so let's go."

"Yes!" I celebrated, punching the air in victory until I noticed that Colden had stopped and was looking past me.

"Doesn't it look like there are fewer traders and vendors this year?" He frowned.

I turned and followed his gaze.

Usually, colorful stalls filled the streets of Pavrenes, as new people and foreign smells visited our island. This time, however, there were only a few stalls scattered sparsely along the streets of the hamlet.

"I wonder what's going on," I mused.

Still holding my hand, he pulled me along as he continued walking.

"Let's just try to make the best of it and still have fun."

The first stall was bright blue and full of art. Paintings hung along the wall while crystal vases and other trinkets sat on the table. Colden browsed through the objects while I stared at the paintings.

The artist brought life to each one with their vibrant colors and bold strokes. My favorite piece was the one with various animals painted gold against a vibrant blue background, while Colden's was the painting of a man's head against an orange background with rain clouds looming above him.

The second stall, 'Merica's Mercantile', was filled with jewelry and spiritual herbs. The lavender scent overpowered all the others, reminding me of home and my mother.

Then, something caught my eye.

A magnificent bracelet made of silver and amethyst that was hanging delicately on a bronze stand.

The salesperson, Merica, had been eyeing me intently since the moment I had walked into her stall. She got off her chair quickly and made her way to the bracelet.

"You like that one, do you? Just got it in. It was made by Fulla Lunaredi herself."

I nodded slowly as if I knew who that was and accepted the bracelet as she placed it gently into my open hands. It gleamed brightly in the sunlight, and the colors looked beautiful against my light brown skin.

I turned the price tag hanging off it and glanced closer.

"What is it?" asked Colden, as I reluctantly set the bracelet back onto the bronze stand.

"It's nice but it would take me months to save and afford such a thing."

He frowned but said nothing more.

With a wave goodbye to Merica, I walked out of the stall, my mind was filled with thoughts of the bracelet, and my nose was flooded with the scent of lavender.

o

Lavender.

The scent still lingered in my fading dream along with thoughts of my missing mother until I realized that I was awake.

My eyes throbbed, so I kept them shut. I was no longer at sea. My hands were bound by rope, and my mouth gagged. The smell of the ocean was replaced by the stench of horses and the gentle rocking of the boat was gone and instead I felt the bumps and vibrations of a cart riding along a dirt road.

Talicia! Where was my sister?

I fought through the pain and opened my eyes, relieved to see Talicia lying next to me. Like me, her hands were bound, and her mouth was gagged. Even though I tried shouting through the gag, her eyes remained closed.

I thought back to the boat and my purple eyes. What had caused it? And why had the pirates collapsed at my gaze?

The cart screeched to a stop and the curtains were yanked back. Light flooded the cart, and as I squinted, I saw that it was the pirate who hijacked our ship.

I yelled, but my sounds were muffled. The man smiled, revealing his gold teeth before leaving.

"Are you sure?"

It was the pirate woman from the *Estonia*.

They'd successfully robbed and kidnapped us, and judging by the bright light outside, the night had passed, and it was at least the next day.

Why were they keeping us alive? The worst-case scenario was that our freedom depended on me, so I began contemplating the best plan of action.

What would Grimke do?

I needed more information to come up with a plan. Were we nearing the Eastern Aid Tower or were we closer to Opulake? Had we gone north instead of west? I tried to picture a map of Damasyr in my head, but I couldn't remember what other settlements bordered the eastern coast.

The cart started moving once again, so I took this opportunity to nudge Talicia awake with my foot. Her eyes burst open after a few kicks. She pulled against the rope and tried screaming through the gag, but it was all in vain.

The air around us changed, as the stench of burning and rotting flesh filled the air. Had there been a fire?

The cart stopped once again, but this time a pair of large grubby hands reached through the curtains and pulled Talicia out of the cart.

I screamed and wiggled, trying to get closer to her. I pushed my head through the curtain which caused my body to fall over the edge of the wagon and onto the ground.

Ignoring the pain, I looked around for Talicia but couldn't spot her. Another pair of arms pulled me up to my feet.

We were nowhere near the Eastern Aid Tower, which meant that we were probably in Opulake.

Opulake was more of a village and was much bigger than Pavrenes, but all the small buildings of the town were either collapsed, vandalized, or currently burning, yet no one seemed concerned with the fires.

Filthy men and women walked the streets, unbothered by the destruction all around them or the fact that a girl was bound and gagged against her will right in front of them.

A large tower like one of the aid towers had its large wooden door breached, yet it was the only structure not significantly damaged.

That would be the Opulaki Aid Tower. Grimke told me once that Lord Laurens lived in this tower. He'd turned it into a lounge, and it was no longer used for aid or emergency supplies.

At the center of the city square was a large pile of dead bodies, some were still burning while others were charred beyond recognition. The scent and sight threw me over the edge. I hunched over, as bile filled my mouth.

I forced myself to take deep breaths and slowed my racing heart. I was still gagged, so vomiting was not an option. I needed to get through this.

The man dragged me down the street, and each time I tried resisting, he slapped me on the back of my head. I tried manifesting the pressure and anger I felt on the *Estonia*, but it wasn't the same.

Nothing happened.

The bandit grinned at me.

"I'm sure you'll put on a good show after what you did on the boat. You shouldn't worry about the girl; she'll fetch a good price somewhere. Focus on yourself."

The bandits who noticed him dragging me cheered in excitement, and the sound of their shouts filled the arena.

"It's a shame that Jesuit isn't here. After what we saw on the boat, I'm sure he would have loved to recruit you. But it matters not; we'll still have fun with you anyway."

I tensed at his words.

There were rumors of Umbari slavers who roamed the streets of Umbar and took anyone who wasn't royal blood as a slave. Could they be sending us there?

"Keep walking," he grunted, forcing me to continue.

There were groups huddled throughout the streets, drinking and arguing over the items they'd looted from pillaged from the dilapidated homes.

I was herded into a nearby building. One side of the building was a crumbled mess, while the other side was untouched. The inside of the lobby was dark and derelict. The man walked through the darkness with ease. He pulled out a key from his pocket and opened the door behind the front desk. There was nothing but darkness beyond the door.

He pushed me forward and I stumbled in blindly, trying to hold on to anything. I felt metal bars. This must be a cell or cage. Pavrenes had extraordinarily little crime in our small hamlet, and we didn't have a prison, but I knew what a jail felt like regardless of that.

The pirate grabbed my hand and cut the rope off my wrists. As I shook my hands free, he thrust a plate into them.

I tried shouting and asking for Talicia, but the gag was still over my mouth.

I pulled it off quickly and ran towards the gate.

"Where is Talicia?" I asked the man, shaking the bars. "Where is my sister?"

He laughed, ignoring my questions as he locked the door.

I screamed at him and kept asking as I tried to reach through the bars and stop him, but he left me alone, in the darkness, with no answers.

Left in solitude with my thoughts, I wondered how I ended up in such a desperate situation.

Grimke was dying, Colden wasn't here to help, Pavrenes was falling, Talicia was missing, Opulake was overrun, and here I was in the dark.

Everything had fallen apart.

I threw the plate aside and dropped to my knees and took a deep breath.

Ever since I took over for Grimke, I'd had to put on a brave face for everyone. Now that I was sitting on the cold floor, all alone, for the first time, I felt I could be vulnerable. I cried, screamed, and heaved until there was nothing left in me.

After some time, my stomach growled loudly, echoing throughout my cell. I searched for the plate, found a piece of stale bread on it, and ravaged it.

I could hear the shouting and screams from outside the building. The bread was nothing compared to Jacob's, but I was starving, and I ate every crumb of it before throwing the plate.

It hit the bars of the cell door and clattered onto the cell floor, but it did not break.

"If you are still hungry, you can have the rest of my food. I don't have much of an appetite for once."

I stopped and looked in the direction of the soft voice. I wasn't alone. Quickly, I wiped my eyes and steadied my breathing.

"Thank you," I said, still embarrassed, "but I don't think this bread is edible."

The girl chuckled in the shadows.

"Who are you?"

"Arabella of Opulake, at your service."

So, we were in Opulake. How long had I been asleep?

"What happened here, Arabella? Where is Lord Laurens?"

"Laurens is dead. He was holding plague tonics in the keep. The people rebelled and were on the brink of victory when a group of bandits attacked and caught both groups off guard. They killed most of the townspeople, and the ones that survived were sent to the arenas to fight to the death with Samson, one of the bandit lieutenants.

If we win, we can claim our freedom, but no one has won against Samson if the guards are to be believed."

Who was this Samson and what made him such a formidable fighter? And if he could defeat every man and woman, how did I stand any chance?

"Where would they have taken someone too small to fight?"

Arabella was quiet for a moment.

"You are asking about your sister, right?" she answered, reluctantly. "If she is not fighting, then most likely she is dead, but I cannot say for sure. I've been here for the last month and had not met anyone who is not a bandit or headed for the arenas."

Dead? My heart dropped and my body shivered. No, Arabella was wrong. If Talicia was dead, I'd know. She couldn't be dead.

"And what happened to Lord Laurens? I mean, how did he die?"

"I am not sure," she said, "but I've heard rumors that he was killed with the Mystio."

"The Mystio? Aren't they the best fighters in the kingdom? I've heard that one Mystio is worth ten fighters."

Mystio were special soldiers trained at the capital separate from the Damasyri military. They were like special forces, and I'd heard that one of them could take on twenty enemies or more at once and win in the end.

"Well, there were Mystio stationed here, yes, but our town is so small that only two Mystio were stationed here. I am sure they put up a fight, but Samson is strong and there were over thirty other bandits. Many of the bandits died, but eventually, both Eufaula and Velma fell. And even if they had won, Samson is submissive to the bandit captain Jesuit, and I have heard there is even another lieutenant who is just as strong as Samson."

I looked around the dark room and listened closely but heard nothing.

"Is there anyone else here?"

"N-no, I am the last. They did not think of me as much of a fighter, so they have saved me for last."

"Well, are you?"

"Never been in a fight, but you never know when your life is on the line."

That may have been true, but it certainly wasn't reassuring. It seemed we were being sent to our deaths as no other Opulakis remained besides Arabella.

"How often are the arena fights?"

"They usually fight every day. There have been a few days when no one was taken, but I think today is my day."

"That's if they don't take me instead," I replied.

"If we are blessed, it will be one of the dual fights, they have done that before. They take two fighters or sometimes even three fighters, but still, no one has returned."

"That could benefit us, though," I said, squinting in the darkness as I tried to size Arabella up.

I stood up and began pacing the perimeter of my cell.

Back in Pavrenes, I'd broken up a couple of small brawls, went hunting, and trained with Grimke. Would that be enough? I'd feel better if I had my sword. Dropping myself to the floor, I leaned back against the wall and closed my eyes.

I am in control of myself.

Grimke would tell me to repeat these words over and over as he taught me how to meditate. After some time, I realized that my breathing was calm, and the negative emotions were beginning to fade. And even though I was still in turmoil, meditating helped me accept them.

Maybe I should do this more often.

My mind wandered to happier times.

Before I was separated from Talicia.

Before my capture.

Before I had to leave Colden behind.

Before Grimke had gotten sick.

Before my mother left.

My mother's face loomed in my mind. She had unrestrained kinky black hair and brown skin like mine, but darker, something I had never seen in Pavrenes. Grimke had fair skin and Talicia had inherited almost none of my mother's complexion. She and Grimke were almost the same shade.

Why did you leave?

That was the question that ran through my mind daily, paired with another question of why she had not returned. She was an important woman; her responsibilities had called her elsewhere. It wasn't her choice. That's what I told myself often and it always made me feel a bit better.

"Get up!"

I jumped up, startled. I must've dozed off. The pirate was standing before me, holding a lantern.

"Come on then, if you want to keep all ten of your fingers," he snarled, the horrid stench of his breath filled the room and made it unbearable.

I wobbled forward, turning back one last time to say goodbye to Arabella. But all the cells were empty.

"Where's the girl that was here?" I asked, as he grabbed my hand and pulled me into the hallway.

He didn't answer. I didn't think he would.

As I was escorted out of the Mystio building, I looked for anything useful. The pirate hadn't bothered binding my hands again, but there were no weapons or anything else that may have been helpful.

My eyes wandered and I thought of making a run for it until I felt something sharp prod me in the back and I jumped in surprise. The pirate had poked me with his blade.

"Don't try nothing."

I nodded and continued faster.

The light of Astria was blinding after being in the dark cell room. Astria was leaning west, soon to follow Zaniah and set, and before long it would be night-time, and I didn't like the idea of fighting with no weapon, no allies, and in the dark.

I thought of Colden. I wish he was here. He always made me feel good. It was easy to be positive with him. I needed some of that right now.

I pictured him in my head and heard him telling a joke. He smiled at me and reached to pull me closer. He could say "I love you" and I would say it back because I knew at that moment, I did.

The sound of a large crowd brought me out of my thoughts.

I wondered if Arabella was fighting already or if she was already dead.

Chapter FOUR

samson

Grimke used to say no one can make you feel small without your permission, but as I was herded into a large building with an open ceiling, I felt pretty insignificant.

Astria was almost completely gone and the violet crest of Ithil was beginning to make an appearance on the opposite horizon.

We entered an old building with rows of pews surrounding a large sand pit at the center. It would've once been a temple devoted to Eloah, but all traces of paintings were gone, and bits and pieces of broken statues were scattered throughout the room.

The place reeked of stale alcohol and sweat, and the pews were crammed with pirates and bandits. Blood soaked the sand, and the pit was fenced by broken pillars depicting Eloah.

When the pirates spotted me, the noise got louder. Many were placing bets while others sneered and shouted insults at me.

"This fight is going to be short!" a portly pirate with a long white beard said.

His short, dumpy friend next to him cackled.

"I bet she'd last five minutes."

They all laughed as they sneered down at me.

"No, she'd last one."

The rest were either too drunk to gamble or impatiently waiting for the fight to begin. The chants and shouts got louder as more bandits saw me.

How could someone put money on human life? They disgusted me.

I locked eyes with a woman who seemed younger than the rest of the bandits. She had piercing grey eyes and watched me without cheering or placing a bet.

I wondered who she was until my escort pushed me forward. I stumbled, and when I looked again, the girl was gone.

Despite my grim predicament, I straightened my back and held my head high. I would win, and then I'd rescue Talicia, and save Grimke. My sister was nowhere in sight, but I did see the woman pirate from the *Estonia.* She waved at me.

51

"Who's the tall lady?" I asked the pirate escorting me.

"Lieutenant Captain Olympia. She's the reason you're still alive."

I was then thrown into the pit.

I coughed, as the sand flew in the air. The crowd leered as I tried to steady myself. A hand reached out, and without thinking, I grabbed it. The girl that helped me had eyes just like mine, and unlike everyone else who was leering and rambunctious, she looked nervous.

"Arabella?"

She nodded, with a grim smile.

"They did not think a fat girl like me was worth much of a fight, so they brought you too," she said, gesturing around us.

The first thing that caught my eye was her hair. Arabella's hair started curly and black before fading into fiery red at the ends. She was even shorter than me and I was already pretty short. She had hazel eyes just like mine that sat behind whimsical full moon glasses, and brown skin that was even darker than mine. She was the first person I had met, excluding my mom, with a darker skin tone.

Arabella's feet were bare, and she wore a dark green dress that reached toward her wrists and forefoot. She was indeed a large girl, but I knew that didn't mean she was weak. I hoped their underestimation of her would be to our advantage.

The air suddenly changed.

"Samson! Samson! Samson!"

The crowd began chanting as a large man emerged on the other end of the sand pit. He was covered in tattoos that gleamed against his pale, shiny skin, which I suspected had been rubbed with oil. His dreaded blond hair fell to the small of his back.

He was tall, over six feet, and compared to us, he was a giant. He wore nothing but a loose loincloth and black leather sandals.

Another man emerged, carrying a horn.

"Welcome," he shouted. "This will be our final fight before we move to the next town."

I stopped breathing at his words.

Pavrenes, I thought.

Arabella and I stood frozen as everything unfolded quickly.

The bell rang and Samson charged toward us with balled fists. We had no weapons, like him. My blood was boiling, though, and I could not afford to fail here; too much was at stake. I would win and I would demand they bring me Talicia.

Samson turned towards Arabella who stood with her feet planted firmly with her hands up, ready to fight. Using this to my advantage, I grabbed the blood-soaked sand from the floor and as he drew nearer, I aimed it at his eyes and tossed it.

Samson howled and cursed as the sand hit its mark. As he rubbed his fist on his eyes, I fired two punches where I hoped his kidneys were. Grimke had taught me the weak spots of the human body, but back then I had shrugged off his battle advice so often, I was surprised I remembered his words.

Hitting Samson felt like punching a large sack of flour back home and as my hands came back, they stung and tingled. He, however, was unaffected. With his eyes red and splotched, he focused his rage on me and charged. I tried to dodge him, but he was fast, and with one slap, my world was spinning. The crowd jeered and roared at Samson's assault.

Samson turned his attention back to Arabella, and I watched in horror as he brought his giant fists down toward her chest.

But Arabella stopped him.

Her body radiated a lime-green energy. I watched as the energy moved swiftly and concentrated on her right arm and stopped Samson's blow with a single hand.

Samson stepped back, shocked for a moment, but at that moment, Arabella took advantage of his surprise. She extended her leg and hooked Samson's foot with her foot. Quickly, she pulled towards herself and caused Samson to fall backward.

The crowd was silent now.

"Arabella," I cried, running over to her. "Are you okay? What was that?"

Before she could answer, Samson groaned and pulled himself off the floor while glaring at Arabella.

"This town seems to be full of Channelers," he snarled, dusting himself off. "I have defeated everyone I've faced so far, and you will be no different, little girl."

Arabella looked at me, her chest rising and descending quickly.

"Kind of hard to explain right now."

Samson charged at us again, and this time, despite Arabella's power, she stumbled for a moment and her power faded.

She looked drained. So, when Samson aimed his next attack at her, I pushed her aside and took the punch in my gut.

I cursed, falling to my knees, and gasping for breath. My midsection burned, but Samson gave me no recess. I was slammed onto my back as Samson kicked me hard on my left arm and my head bounced on the sand with two muffled thuds.

I wheezed and strained to sit up. My ribs screamed from the action and set my nerves on fire.

Something caught my eye next to me. Lying in the sand was a copper star with a swan engraved atop. It must've belonged to a Mystio; the swan was their symbol. I grabbed it and rolled just as Samson tried to stomp my head with his giant foot.

As I rolled, I slashed the star at him. Blood quickly followed, letting me know my attack had pierced his skin, but I didn't have time to see how much damage I'd done. I kept rolling away.

Samson began stomping hard on Arabella with his uninjured leg. Arabella herself was in the sand, stuck in the fetal position.

Although Samson was putting his full weight behind his foot, Arabella's arms and legs were cloaked in that lime-green energy again.

I launched myself and slammed my shoulder into him. He snapped around quickly and threw a punch my way, but I dodged it just in time.

With his ankle now exposed, I aimed a kick and hit my mark. He lurched over in pain, and before he could catch himself, I punched him square on his nose which made a satisfying *crunch*.

Blood flowed from his nostrils as he howled. His long nose erupted with redness and was now crooked. Samson blinked hard and held his eyes shut for a moment.

Arabella!

I ran over and dropped to the ground beside her. Her eyes remained closed, but luckily her chest was moving. She was still alive.

"Arabella," I called, shaking her arm.

She opened her eyes and looked up at me, confused. I rose and quickly helped her off the ground. She wrapped her arm around my shoulder and leaned against me.

I glanced back at Samson who was hunched over in pain. He shook his head, sending blood flying onto the ground.

"We've got him on the ropes," I said to Arabella, and she followed my gaze.

"I cannot say that I share your opinion," she said, with a heavy breath, "but I envy your optimism."

"Tell me how you're doing that glowing thing?"

"It is Elohan Faith Magic, I am surprised you have not heard of it. Mages, Channelers, Elohans, Djinni, Warlocks-"

"How do you do it?" I asked, cutting her off.

We were running out of time. Samson was now staggering towards us with a mad gleam in his green eyes. He was injured, but ready for more.

"Feelings, intent, and faith."

"I fought another of your kind," sneered Samson, revealing his blood-soaked teeth. "He died quickly and on his knees. Pathetic sight, it was. A holy man, who was crying out for his pathetic god."

Arabella froze beside me.

"What was his name again?" he continued taunting. "Tripa Farce?"

Arabella stepped forward with her fists up, but this time, though, Samson was too fast. Before she could summon her Faith Magic, Samson kneed her in the gut, causing her to lurch over and vomit in the sand in front of Samson.

"No!" I cried.

I ran to her as she fell onto the sandy arena floor. Samson turned his death stare on me. I tried to slow down, but I couldn't, and he bashed me on the head as the crowd cheered on.

The sounds of the crowd faded, and the world turned dark.

o

I woke up crying because of the pain that seared through my head. It took a few moments for all my memories to come rushing back, and my body froze with dread as I remembered where I was.

Both Astria and Zaniah had set and the light of Ithil bathed us in its purple light. In the middle of the sand pit, I was suspended off the ground, staring at the crowd. Samson was holding me up in the air by my twin braids.

He lifted me higher and spun around, showing me to the crowd surrounding us. My scalp screamed in agony and so did I.

"Samson, Samson, Samson," the crowd chanted.

Arabella was nearby, lying unconscious in the sand. Her green dress was mostly in tatters, revealing long scars that covered her back.

How old were the scars? I wondered. They didn't look recent, but I wondered if the bandits tortured her. Were they torturing Talicia?

"The child is here!" the announcer jeered. "Now kill the girl."

Next to the announcer stood Olympia, holding Talicia by her side. I fought and wiggled, but I was no match for Samson's raw strength.

As I struggled, Samson took his left hand, releasing my hair, and wrapped it around my neck.

I felt the muscles in my throat being squeezed and my breathing was restricted. It was hard to focus on anything but the pain and Talicia.

They had brought her to me, now all I had to do was win. It would be a task easier said than done. She appeared untortured, and for the moment, unharmed.

Talicia tried to fight off her captors and run to me, but it did no good. They threw her to the ground and one of the captors slapped her.

Anger shot through my body, numbing the pain and filling me with rage. I thought back to Arabella's words and tried to summon the Elohan Faith Magic.

Faith was a concept I'd never given much thought to. It was always Grimke and myself protecting everyone we loved, so I did not need to depend on a higher power.

Feelings. Intent. Faith.

As the rage grew inside me, I felt the familiar pressure building within me.

"Release me," I screamed. "Now!"

Samson surprised himself, as he released his vice grip on my neck and let me fall to the floor. I felt his grip loosening and tried to catch myself, but my legs failed me, and I fell into a clump on the ground.

I steadied myself as Samson recovered from his trance and swung at me. His fist struck me hard on my head, causing me to stagger back.

Feelings. Intent. Faith.

I tried dodging his blows while struggling to focus my energy. The thundering pain echoed through my body, and I focused on the feeling of that pain.

I gasped as a thin layer of purple energy coated my arms and held my arms together like a makeshift shield, but a punch from Samson quickly shattered the aura arm guards and bruised my skin.

Come on. Feelings. Intent. Faith, but faith in what? Faith in myself?

I could win.

I had to win.

I will win.

The purple aura appeared once more in wisps before solidifying. I winced as Samson's fist slammed into the aura bracers, but they withstood the blow, and with each following blow, the aura got thicker until I could no longer feel the attack.

"Another Elohan," Samson snarled. "I've fought many of you, the change of color doesn't matter. The problem with you Elohans is that you don't use your power for offense! What a waste!"

As he aimed his punch at my gut, I willed my energy to move from my hand to my gut. The vibrations traveled from my arm to my gut and protected me.

I got it to work. I can save Talicia.

My arms shimmered with the magic, and I grasped it. I pulled my arms back and threw them forward. The energy left my fingers and formed a shimmering purple aura shaped like a wall.

I had hoped the wall would protect me like the bracers, but Samson aimed a heavy kick at the wall, and when his foot slammed into the wall, the aura broke apart with a loud sound like shattering glass.

The pieces faded away before hitting the ground. The force from the aura wall shattering threw Samson onto his knees.

My body no longer felt pain. I was calm, like earlier in the day when I had meditated in my cell. I was in full control at that moment.

I Channeled the purple aura to my left foot and kicked Samson with everything I had. The aura shattered once more, but again; I felt no pain.

The force sent me crashing onto my butt, but I scrambled to my feet quickly. My legs felt like noodles, but after a moment, I was back in fighting form. I tasted blood in my mouth and realized I had bit my tongue when I'd fallen.

Samson howled, writhing on the floor. He did not look so formidable now. He was no giant, just a regular man.

"You'll pay for this!"

I Channeled my energy for more, ready for his attack. I was full of newfound confidence, but moments later, his body went still.

I stepped back once and then carefully moved closer, watching his arms for sudden movements. I did not want him to get me if he was playing possum.

Was he dead?

Dread filled me at this thought. I couldn't be a killer. I couldn't be one of them. As I got closer and inspected him, I sighed with relief. He was still breathing.

My aura had dissipated, and though I tried to bring it back in preparation for any other attacks, it wouldn't come.

I turned to the silent crowd, ready to fight. Could you trust the word of murderers and thieves?

I attempted to steel myself and I tried to look at every member of the First Constellation at once. I looked for Olympia and the girl with the grey eyes I'd seen previously, but both were hidden from me.

I gestured toward Samson's body in the sand and cleared my throat.

"Who's next?"

The crowd erupted in a deafening roar of celebration.

We had won.

Chapter FIVE

estella

I stood in disbelief, staring at the defeated man before me, and thought back to Grimke's advice.

Believing is half the battle. But remember, it's important to recognize your level of skill and retreat if necessary.

Today, retreating wasn't an option, and without Arabella's help and the Elohan Faith Magic, my skills alone wouldn't have been enough.

Though I'd never thought much of the god Eloah before today, I owed him. I clasped my hands together and closed my eyes.

Thank you for saving me and my sister.

After my quick prayer of thanks, I searched once more for Olympia, but she had fled, it seemed. I heard someone shout something unclear to me and suddenly the bandits began to rush for the exits of the makeshift arena.

I had been worried that they'd go back on their rumored claims of freedom, but as they fled, they paid us little attention.

I turned to face Talicia. She had been released by her captors. Talicia threw herself on me, and the force of her sent us both into the blood-stained sand. I wrapped my arm around her with my good arm and pulled her as close as I could.

"Are you okay?" I asked, as she sobbed in my arms.

She nodded in between the tears and squeezed tighter. I was glad she was okay and she appeared uninjured.

"You beat him," she said, in awe. "I can't believe it."

"It wasn't *that* hard, but thanks for the vote of confidence," I said, and she laughed.

A cough brought us out of our reunion. Arabella was awake and at the sound of her cough I looked over and saw her slowly picking herself up off the floor.

She exhaled deeply and stretched her arms above her head. She saw us looking at her and smiled at us meekly as she slowly staggered towards us.

I started to smile back but suddenly my heart began throbbing painfully in my chest, while my brain felt as though it was trying to burst through my skull. I lurched over as my entire body spasmed in pain. My entire body felt like it was on fire.

"I don't feel so good," I told Arabella, as she stood beside me with a worried expression.

Talicia was holding onto me and rubbing my back gently as I spat blood on the arena floor. The world started spinning, and my legs turned to jelly as I fell into the sand.

Talicia dropped to the floor and placed my head on her lap. She began whispering words of comfort, although I could see the fear in her eyes. I smiled weakly as I looked up at her. No matter what happened to me, she was all right. My sister was free.

Sadly, I had failed my mission. I'd never get the tonics to Pavrenes. I'd never see Colden again. Grimke would die. Colden would die. And everyone else in Pavrenes would soon follow.

I hoped Arabella would at least take care of Talicia. I had no idea how she would get home. Maybe Colden would come for her.

Arabella's head appeared above me, and I felt her fingers poking and prodding me as her mouth moved. She was singing a hymn of some kind.

"Protect Talicia," I managed to croak.

Arabella continued singing as I drifted in and out of consciousness. She lifted her hands, which were now cloaked in her neon green aura, and placed them gently on my chest.

My purple aura glowed and met her touch. Arabella's magic began to cover her entire body, and as it did, my aura mimicked hers and cloaked me in purple energy.

A sharp pain pierced my heart, and slowly, everything faded to black.

o

I opened my eyes and stared around in awe.

I was sitting on a pew in the Opulaki Temple of Eloah. The arena was gone, and the temple was restored and pristine.

The pew's white marble gleamed against the sun's rays that filtered into the temple skylights. Beautiful paintings of Elohan scenes lined the walls. I saw one that depicted a large boat of some sort under a black sky surrounded by stars.

Was I dead?

"Excuse me, Arabella," said a woman in green.

The woman in green moved past me and sat further down on the pew. The temple was full to the brim, and everyone wore a sash of solid neon green. I tried looking back but I couldn't.

What did she mean by *Arabella?*

My body was restrained, and the only thing I could move was my toes. My feet were bare, so wiggling my toes in the sand gave me some comfort but after a moment I realized they were moving independently of my control.

I felt claustrophobic and drained. My forehead began throbbing uncomfortably. I tried fighting it but the mental wall I put up was slowly faltering.

Odessa, relax!

Where had that voice come from? I tried to look around, but my neck refused to move. The voice sounded like Arabella's, but she was nowhere in sight.

Relaxing felt impossible at that moment, but I thought back to Grimke and his meditation teachings. I attempted to take control of my breathing, but I could not grasp it.

There was someone else in my consciousness. I was not alone. I could feel Arabella in my mind like a cool and calm wave of water. She didn't freeze or overpower me, yet I felt uneasy about sharing my mind with her.

What are you doing in my mind, Arabella?

I had to form an empathy link to save your life. The empathy link allowed me to give you some of my life energy. You had expended too much of your own. If I had not interfered, you would have surely died.

I thought over her words, as her thoughts and feelings intermingled with my own. Empathy link? Did it have something to do with the Elohan Faith Magic? Was I really dying?

An empathy link is when two or more people are linked through Elohan Faith Magic. Our souls are linked, and our minds can become one, as they are now. We can communicate, meet in a mindscape, or share memories, as long as we both have magic available and are on the same plane. When you use Elohan Faith Magic, you take your feelings and meld them into something. Elohans are taught to only use it for defense, but even that is draining. I have never seen anyone use their aura like I heard you did in the arena.

It was interesting information. I had never heard of anything such as what she had described. I wondered why our auras were different colors if we were both using the Elohan Faith Magic.

The aura you see when you manifest your Faith is your life force personified, your soul, and everyone has a distinct color. They can be similar colors but no two are exactly the same. Over time it recharges, but if you expend too much magic, your body and mind will lose energy and you will die. You lack the training required to rely on magic alone in combat.

Grimke had trained me to fight using my strength and skills. This was something new, and every answer I received sprouted two more questions.

Why can't I move? Where are we?

The cool wave continued crashing over me, as silence momentarily filled my mind. Arabella was there, but she was distracted by something else. So, I listened to the waves and waited.

This is a memory of mine. Neither of us can truly move. We are one person in this moment and events will play out as they did then. We are both unconscious while my magic attempts to replenish you. Both of our bodies need time to recover. This is one from my perspective although I would prefer you not-

Wait, wait wait, I thought, ignoring the feeling of waves, and focusing on her words. *What do you mean by attempt? Is this not sure?*

We must find equilibrium. Our souls must align, and if we are incompatible, you will die, and most likely so will I.

What does having our souls linked mean?

It is what allows us to communicate like this, but more importantly if one of us dies, the other dies too. There are other links like it, but this was the only one that I thought would save you.

I fell silent at her words and thought back to my life in Pavrenes. So much had changed since then. I'd had to fight for my life and Talicia's, I'd discovered a part of myself that I never knew existed, and now, I was holding someone else's life in my hands.

I need to get stronger. If anything happened to Arabella, my sister would have no one to protect her.

If you want to train your aura, think of it like a muscle, the more you use it, the stronger it will get and the easier it will be to control. It starts with learning to control your breathing, faith, emotions, and intent.

Those words sounded like Grimke's. He'd often preach patience and self-control. It was one of the reasons that he taught me meditation. He'd often say that peace was something within us always, and it could be found anywhere through meditation.

Although Arabella was quiet, something within her had shifted. The cool waves were no longer calming. She was anxious, and not about saving me, she was anxious about us being in this memory.

"Arabella," a man called.

I realized that the man was speaking to me. Glancing down, I saw that my skin was darker and my body bigger. I was also wearing a green dress with a neon green sash. The old man was talking to Arabella, and I was in her body.

The man looked to be a bit younger than Grimke but not by much. He had light brown eyes and unnaturally brown hair. His face had wrinkles that were covered with a layer of makeup.

"Would you care to demonstrate? People of Eloah, Arabella is the best Morale we have, even better than me. We will watch her progression with great anticipation. Her Faith is as big as she is."

I rose to my feet and took his hand nervously. As we moved, Tripa Fons's robe shifted and revealed dark, fancy leather boots. I followed him up the sandy aisle and onto the raised stage at the center.

71

The flame of Eloah hissed at me as I passed it, and its green flames reached out and touched me. I had never seen green flames, and if I had control of Arabella's body, I would have stopped to inspect it further. I wanted to know why it was green.

That flame had been lit for a thousand years before the bandits came here and destroyed much of our town. Look at these people, they are all dead.

Arabella's voice had returned to my mind, and she was in pain.

Is this the man Samson was talking about?

Yes, the man was Tripa Fons, the religious leader of Opulake. He was on par with Lord Laurens as far as status went. He also raised Estella and I for most of our teenage years.

It must be horrible losing one's father this way. I know the pain I felt when I found out Grimke had the plague, and I couldn't imagine what I'd feel if I lost him altogether.

How long will we be out?

As long as it takes for us to get in sync.

Standing at the altar, was Estella. She crossed her arms and scowled at me as I approached.

"Estella, are you ready?" asked Tripa Fons.

Estella nodded and crossed the altar to meet me, holding two daggers in her hands. She stood tall at five foot five, much taller than me. She had dark grey eyes and long black hair with a ghostly streak of white flowing at her roots above her forehead. She had full lips with red lipstick.

She wore amethyst earrings and a necklace that glittered with the light from the flame of Eloah. I couldn't see much else as Arabella hung her head and stared at the floor as she waited for Estella.

"Estella is our second-best Morale. She will demonstrate an attack on Arabella who will use her Faith to protect herself. This will demonstrate how we all can rely on Eloah to protect us; all we need is the faith to believe in him."

Estella's scowl deepened, though Tripa Fons didn't notice as he'd turn his focus to the congregation. Like Samson, he was an entertainer.

She sheathed her daggers and lifted her hands. She looked as if I had seen her before, but she was not from Pavrenes. Maybe I had seen her in my dreams, but I thought I would have familiarized anyone with hair like hers.

She was supposed to hit me in the stomach. We rehearsed it several times. She was to hit me, and I was to repel the blow with my Faith

Arabella lifted her head and turned to the congregation. I finally got a closer look at the crowd, who were whispering with each other. They were talking about Arabella, and it was clear that she hated being the center of attention.

I felt her nervousness through Arabella in my mind, even though she should have known how the demonstration would turn out.

"I will be still, for I know you are with me," whispered Arabella. Moments later, her faith manifested, and she focused it on her stomach. As her gut glowed green, Arabella nodded at Estella.

Estella let out a low growl and punched Arabella hard in the shoulder.

Ouch!

My shoulder ached and the green aura disappeared. Tripa Fons quickly made his way toward us.

"What are you doing, girls?" he snarled. He raised his right hand ever so slightly, and both Estella and Arabella flinched. "Do the demonstration right or I'll beat you both."

His anger suddenly transfigured into a warm smile as he turned back to the crowd and addressed them in a soothing tone.

"Apologies, Elohans, you all know how our dear, Arabella is. Great as she is, big crowds are a bit much for her. Give us but a moment and we will correctly depict Eloah's divine protection."

Things were going terribly, and worry washed over Arabella as she struggled to bring forth her Elohan Faith Magic again. Estella glared at her, waiting impatiently.

I felt Arabella's deep breathing as she focused and recited the prayer of faith once again. The green aura returned, and she focused it on her stomach, but this time, she was sweating profusely.

She nodded at Estella who punched her gut, whose blow was repelled by Arabella's neon green Faith as planned. But this time, I felt Arabella losing her energy as fatigue crept in.

For a second, Estella's face flashed with concern as Arabella dropped to her knees. Tripa Fons walked over to her and gripped her arms tightly.

"What a bow! Look! Look how Eloah will protect you! You need only the Faith!" he preached, ignoring the pain that Arabella was feeling, "Stay loyal to Eloah-"

Tripa Fons was suddenly cut off and he and the world around us turned black. I felt the pain and hurt emanating from within, as Arabella anticipated what was about to come next.

Arabella opened her eyes. I saw she was sitting in a cold, dark cellar. Light flickered from the lone candle, sitting on the floor. Arabella wasn't scared or confused. She knew this place. She'd been here before.

"You did well today, child, but Estella, that brat will be whipped."

Tripa Fons paced the room calmly, caressing a worn black leather whip. Arabella's heart quickened at the sight of it.

"Please do not whip her," Arabella pleaded, looking down at the floor. "She just misses her parents. We both do."

He stopped and turned to face her. Her heart fluttered in fear as she kept her eyes on the whip.

"Yes, the mission trip has gone on much longer than planned, but the journey across the ocean to Tyvent is far, and finding an *imperi* is no small task. Both your parents left you in my care and it's my job to build two strong women of Eloah, and when you act out, you will be disciplined. You girls failed my demonstration today and now someone is getting whipped."

As Tripa Fons glided across the cellar and towards the exit, I felt the fear and resolve build within Arabella as she got up and stumbled towards him.

"Please," she whispered, clutching the sleeve of his shirt. "If someone must be whipped, let it be me. It was my fault. I should have been able to move my Faith to repel her first blow."

Tripa Fons shook off her touch, shaking her hand off him. But as he looked at her closer, something else sparkled in his eyes. I felt Arabella's urge to step back, but she bravely stood in place.

"You would take her lashes?"

She nodded.

Arabella turned and I got a better glimpse of the cellar. There was one tattered sheet laying on the floor and a stack of dusty old books. Arabella longed to curl up and be alone in the darkness. This was her home.

She kneeled with her back to him, and her head bowed. Slowly, she removed her shirt, and I felt the trepidation building as she waited. This wasn't the first time she'd done this. She knew what was coming, and I felt her fear.

Tripa Fons remained silent, and the room remained heavy and cold. That moment felt eternal and, in some way, peaceful, despite her pounding heart.

Whoosh, crack!

I could hear the whip splitting the air and the pain seared my back as it made contact with her skin. It reached from her left to right and a long arc, and even after Tripa Fons pulled back the whip, Arabella's back still stung from the lash.

Whoosh, crack!

The force and pain were too much. It felt more precise and deeper than anything Samson had done to me in the arena.

Arabella fell forward crying in agony and shoved a clump of her blanket into her mouth and bit down on it. I did not know how she endured it, but I was a prisoner in her body.

Whoosh, crack!

"Did you only plan on taking half of her lashes?" Tripa Fons asked as Arabella forced herself onto her feet and backed against the wall, shivering.

At his words, Arabella shook her head and slowly knelt back down in front of the bed.

Whoosh, crack!

I felt the whip dig into Arabella's skin once more and we collapsed in a heap in front of the bed. I knew she would survive this as it was a memory, but I did not know how much more any person could take.

"Rise up," Tripa Fons said, and amazingly Arabella's body rose once more.

Whoosh, crack!

I felt like I was on fire as the pain spread its way throughout Arabella's entire body. Still, she remained standing despite her cries of pain.

She was dying; it felt like being burned alive over and over until there was nothing left but ashes. And I was frozen within her, unable to save the person that was saving me.

Chapter SIX

grimke

"Ready yourselves."

I turned towards Grimke, who was standing before me, waiting. Today, like every day, was training day, and we were doing it at the edge of Queenslen Forest. The summer breeze swept through the shaded area, as both suns shined brightly above us. This was my favorite weather.

My win conditions were aligned perfectly, so this time, I was going to win. The weather was fair, I was rested, and Talicia was in high spirits.

Half the time she didn't want to train, and the other half, she would rather die than be excluded from a training session. Today she was in the latter mood.

I usually did not get the option on whether I would do our training, but Grimke claimed he gave Talicia the choice because she was younger, but I wasn't much older when he'd begun training me.

"Stay behind me," I instructed.

Talicia and I held old short swords that were so blunted they could do little damage even if we *could* tag Grimke, which had never happened, but I felt, for the moment, confident at our chances.

Talicia pouted at my words but followed my instruction. Grimke was holding a wooden practice sword. To him, it was a handicap, but that's what he needed to use if we were to stand a fighting chance. I hated the handicap, but we needed it.

I carefully stepped forward, while Grimke nodded in encouragement. While I lowered my blade in defense, he held his sword high. With one swift motion, I swung my sword low, but Grimke intercepted my attack with little effort and switched to offense.

He pushed forward quickly with no hesitation and jabbed toward me. I anticipated his attack and attempted to catch his blade with my own and deflect it, but he was stronger than me.

I had managed to slow his jab, but he pushed his blade against mine suddenly, and I lost my balance and stumbled backward.

Grimke waited as I caught my breath and re-evaluated my plan of attack. Although this wasn't a real fight, I didn't want Grimke going easy on me.

I was already breathing heavily, and it seem today wasn't my day again. If I was going to lose anyway, there was one other thing I could do; something I hadn't tried before.

"You ready?" I whispered to Talicia.

Her face brightened and she nodded enthusiastically. She gripped her short sword tightly and planted her feet.

You did all this as a kid? No wonder you are such a good fighter.

Arabella's voice startled me. And then I remembered. We were still linked, and she was trying to save me. Only now, we were in my memories, not hers.

She hadn't spoken since her memory had ended and we had shifted into one of mine. I could tell reliving the memory had shaken her.

Are we still dreaming? Why are we in my memories?

Yes, we are still dreaming but this is good because we have entered phase two.

There are phases to our empathy link. As relieved as I was that we'd completed the first phase, I wondered how many phases we had left.

There are two phases in total, Odessa. But once phase two is completed and successful, we will wake up.

In my memories, Grimke was still staring at us with a small smile. He was the best swordsman or woman on the island, and since the day I turned ten, we'd been training daily.

Talicia always insisted on tagging along, but she was more of a handicap than an advantage because Grimke's winning condition was that he only had to best one of us.

He reasoned that if we defeated someone but lost a sister that was no real victory. It made sense, I'd go crazy if I lost my sister, but Talicia being there made it easier to lose.

But we were ready now. Talicia and I started our attack. I went in first with Talicia in my shadow. Grimke parried both our blades just as I'd expected.

Grimke once taught us that whenever we're facing more than one opponent, the best option is to separate and disarm one of them.

So, as I expected, after blocking Talicia's sword, he moved in close and twisted his blade around my wrist, I let him disarm me, even though I was unsure if I could have stopped it anyway.

All part of the plan. Watch this, Arabella.

My sword fell to the ground with a small thud, and I quickly bent down to pick it up. This left me vulnerable to Grimke's attack, but it was part of the plan. Instead of grabbing my sword alone, I also grabbed a handful of sand.

Before Grimke's blade could tap my exposed back, Talicia's blade caught his. With him momentarily distracted by Talicia, I shot up and tossed the sand in the air, aiming it at Grimke's face.

That moment of distraction was exactly what we needed for Talicia to bypass his weakened defense and touch her blade to his chest.

"Tag," we said, together.

We'd won.

You do like your sand.

As I thought about Arabella's funny quip, the memory faded, and we were transported to another point in that day.

It was late in the evening, and though Zaniah had set, it was still as hot as earlier on. Grimke and I were sitting in the kitchen while Talicia napped in the front room.

I sat by the table while Grimke dried the dishes. Our dining table hadn't seen much action since my mother left. It was now used for storage.

I was drawing a portrait using charcoal, and right now, I was struggling with the nose. Noses were the bane of my existence.

"You did well today," Grimke said without looking at me.

I looked up from my drawing and grinned at my father with pride. Grimke was very selective with his praise, so I held onto every word and enjoyed the moment.

He didn't turn around or speak further, so I turned back to my drawing. It was a sketch of my mother, Moesha. I had many sketches of her as she was my most prominent muse.

But mostly I was afraid that if I stopped, I'd forget how she looked, even though I often saw her in my dreams. One day I wouldn't dream of her, and without these portraits, I would forget her visage.

"There's something for you in the front room on the table," Grimke said, interrupting my focus.

"What is it?" I asked.

I got up quickly, unable to hide the grin on my lips and the skip in my step as I hurried to the front room. I hadn't received a gift from anyone since my last birthday. Sitting on the table, elegant and gleaming, was a dark sword.

My sword! This was the day I got my sword from Grimke.

"It's beautiful," I whispered in awe, as I gently lifted it and turned it over.

It was the most elaborate sword I'd ever seen. The scabbard was wrapped in a delicate black and gold design of symbols, or perhaps a foreign language.

That scabbard is probably at the bottom of the ocean or holding some pirate's rusty sword, I thought bitterly. Arabella whispered condolences, as we both felt the joy engulfing me at that moment.

I yanked the sword out of the scabbard and examined it in awe. The blade was short like our practice blades and made of black, gleaming metal. The hilt was made of the same material and wrapped with coils of black leather. I slashed it in the air, and only then did I notice the small amethyst gem at the bottom of the hilt that kept the blade from being completely black.

I swung it in the air until Grimke appeared and sent me outside. I rushed out, with a sheepish smile. I couldn't help but squeal with joy as I slashed through the Pavreni air.

It was perfect.

"Happy Birthday," said Grimke, as he leaned against the doorway and studied me. "You're a woman now. I've done my best to teach you everything I know, and there is nothing left."

I beamed back at him.

"I love it. Thank you, Grimke."

He winced, like he always did, every time I said his first name. I'd promised that I'd only call him dad or father when he stopped keeping secrets. Grimke knew where my mother was, I knew he did, but every time I asked, he refused to give me an answer or would change the subject.

"Does the sword have a name?"

Many great swords had names like people or places did. Bentley, the hamlet bard, told me once about the sword *Sithos* which was said to be forged in sunfire and the great hero Alekisanit wielded the fire of Zaniah through it.

Barnabas, our hamlet stargazer, once showed me the constellation of the general Callyssia and her sword *Kurama* which was said to grant wishes.

"Not one worth carrying with you. It's yours now, so you should give it a name."

I still haven't named that sword. It hasn't done anything legendary except decapitating a practice dummy.

I held up the sword and watched it gleam against Ithil's purple glow.

"With this, I'll have no problem tagging you going forward."

"Teamwork," he countered, wagging his finger at me. "There was a reason I allowed Talicia to join us and gave her a sword in the first place."

I glanced through the open doorway and at Talicia, who was still napping on the lounge chair.

"She's just a kid and it was my plan." I pouted.

"I know she is just a kid. That is why I do not force her to join us. I wanted to do things differently with her. She does not need the training you did," Grimke said, placing his hand on my shoulder.

"Because I'm older?" I asked, looking up at him.

"In part, but my point is, you will surpass me one day, but in the meantime, you'll need to swallow that pride of yours. Is your independence worth the victory?"

"It's not the same, it feels like a sour victory," I said, pulling away from his hand.

"But it is still a victory."

I remained silent as Grimke's words echoed in my mind. The scene faded, and the last thing I saw was his dark blue eyes until they faded too.

o

I woke up and found myself laying in the most comfortable bed I'd ever lain in. It definitely outdid the beds of Pavrenes by a long shot. I was cocooned under several sheets and a fluffy blue blanket.

As I sat up, I was surprised by how revitalized I felt. I twisted and turned my arms, examining each one closely. There was no blood or bruises, and I felt no pain or soreness. The empathy link with Arabella had worked, and I felt the best I ever did in years.

Natural light flooded into the room, and it smelled like lemon peels. I lifted the blankets off of me and swung my legs to the edge of the bed and sighed.

"Odessa! You're awake!"

Talicia jumped off the lavish orange chair on the other side of the room and hopped on the bed beside me.

"Are you okay?" she asked, her features relaxing with relief.

"I am," I said, still flexing my muscles and expecting pain to appear. "How long have I been asleep?"

"Three whole days," Talicia replied, holding up her fingers. "You must have been tired as a dog."

"What?" I gasped.

Three days!

I jumped off the bed and ran towards the door.

"Odessa," huffed Talicia, as she followed me to the door. "Where are you going?"

I turned to her as I continued running.

"The tonics! We need to get them and return to Pavrenes before Grimke and everyone else dies."

The bedroom opened to a long, wide hallway with lofty ceilings. Ornate paintings hung on the wall, depicting different people and landscapes.

If I had the time, I would have loved to have studied them, but instead, I ignored them. I entered a hallway that had a large picture depicting a king with a large city made of white stone in its background.

"Go left," Talicia shouted.

I turned left and ran into a large chamber room. The ceilings were high and made of intricately carved wood. Large copper lanterns hung from the ceiling, casting light on a long wooden table with white velvet chairs.

There was one elevated seat that stood above all, and that was the lord's throne. And next to the throne was Arabella. She wore a beautiful green dress with a delicate white pattern. Like me, Arabella looked refreshed and healed. There were no bruises or blood from our previous fight.

Two Mystio men stood beside her. They wore the signature black uniform and leather boots. Although the one currently talking to Arabella was also wearing a long black cape with a popped-up collar and gold epaulets on each shoulder with a gold swan on the face of each epaulet.

The other Mystio was staring out the window. I followed his gaze and saw the ruined village of Opulake, and I realized we were in the Opulake Aid Tower.

We were on the tallest floor, and it was here where the emergency beacon would be located in case it needed to be lit, but it looked like the tower had indeed been converted to a lavish lounging area.

It was clear the bandits of the First Constellation had been here as much of the eloquence was diminished by filth, damage, and blood.

I stepped into the room and Arabella looked up at the sound of my footsteps. She smiled at me as I approached her and the Mystio.

I am glad you are well, I heard her say in my mind. It would take much time for me to get used to her cool presence in my head.

The man who had been speaking with Arabella crossed the room and stopped before me. I bowed my head as he gripped my forearm tightly.

"My thanks to you," he said, as his black eyes pierced me. "The Mystio stationed here, I'm told, were slain by the bandit lieutenant, Samson, and I'm told he was defeated by the two of you."

He spoke slowly and chose his words carefully. Now that he was so closer, I realized that he was much younger than I first thought. He had sharp cheekbones and neatly loc'd black hair with a few stray strands hanging on his forehead.

His irises were indeed black or at least a very dark brown. As I inspected him, I saw that the whites of his eyes were tinged with redness and bloodshot as if he had been crying.

"Let me introduce myself," he said, raising his hand out. "My name is Lancer Savant Solace. My squad was dispatched here after we received news of a bandit attack, but by the time we arrived, the town had already been lost."

Lancer Savant Solace

In Damasyr, many went without surnames as they were reserved for certain bloodlines. Some Damasyri gave themselves surnames, but the created surnames held little social weight unless there was power or money associated with the given name.

The Queen could give a last name, as a reward or payment, but that rarely happened. Savant had a last name *and* a title. He must have been especially important.

My family had no last name. No one in Pavrenes did. Colden said his grandfather told him that at one point, his family had a last name, but couldn't remember what it was.

A badge was pinned to Savant's belt that spelled Mystio under the swan, and there was a nameplate on his chest with the same word. It was different from the star I found in the sand pit.

"Arabella and I were a team; I couldn't have done it without her."

Savant chortled.

"That's the same thing she told me, only reversed. We need more humble people like the both of you in this world."

Though I had more questions, Arabella caught my eye and shook her head frantically behind Savant, her expression serious.

Please, give him a moment, he can help you, Arabella said through our empathy link, so I decided to hold my tongue.

"One of the Mystio stationed here, Eufaula O'Conner," continued Savant, "she was my *inamorata*. I wanted to thank you personally for defeating her murderer, Lieutenant Samson of the First Constellation. When she died, I fell unconscious for two days, and although Eufaula and I were able to live out her final spiritual moments, I am distraught because I wasn't by her side during her final physical moments."

"And we would've been here with time to spare, if not for the dawdling of the Queen, but as usual she was too concerned with the heirlooms of my kinfolk. Now we have lost Eufaula and Velma, both great Mystio," the other Mystio said.

The other Mystio turned to face us with a scowl on his face. Savant frowned at the outburst, but again, he was slow and careful with his words.

"We serve the Queen, Adonis. We don't want our new friends to get the wrong idea. Treason is a hard charge to disprove, and with the rising fear of rebellion, we don't need additional problems."

These words held no power over him. He walked towards us with the same disapproving look. Unlike Savant, the accessories and badges on Adonis's uniform were silver.

Adonis didn't bother to introduce himself, instead, he focused his gaze on me. I felt self-conscious as he studied me. It felt as though he was sizing up my strengths and weaknesses.

Adonis was as tall as Savant with deep brown skin and eyes. On his forehead was a tattoo in the shape of a red diamond between both of his eyebrows.

Light footsteps approached and we all stopped as Talicia appeared beside me.

"Of course, you're right," Adonis said after a minute of silence.

I didn't have time for their politics. I came to Opulake for a reason, and time was running out.

"I need to gather as many tonics as I can to take back to my village."

Savant hesitated and turned to Arabella, before looking back at me. Adonis remained unfazed.

"While you were unconscious, Adonis and I, along with my other subordinate, Micah, captured many of the remaining bandits and took inventory of this town. As I told Arabella, who asked on your behalf, we did not find tonics of any sort. If there were any, they aren't here any longer."

I cursed silently and began pacing.

What next?

There was a settlement called Drie, but it was even farther west, and by the time I'd go there and return home, Grimke would most likely be dead.

I could go back to the Eastern Aid Tower and check for tonics there, but that would be backtracking, and if there weren't any in stock, my journey to Drie would be even longer.

Either option was a huge gamble, and I was already so short on time.

"The Queen's alchemists and doctors did create a plagicine, though," added Savant. "It's a medicine made to counteract the disease. We have a crate here with us, but policy says we need to transport these bandits to the nearest fort first, which is Fort Mudo, and we would need to do that before we can travel to Pavrenes and distribute the cure."

"I need that plagicine. My village needs that plagicine. People will die if I don't bring it back. I've already been here too long!"

Savant opened his mouth to speak, but Adonis spoke first.

"We both know what the policy says, but Odessa and Arabella have done us a service. This town is dead, why should another town die when we can prevent it?"

Savant bit his lip and fell silent as he thought over Adonis's words.

"How about this," started Adonis, as he looked from me to Savant, "you and Micah take Samson and any bandits you can to Fort Mudo, while I escort Odessa to Pavrenes with the plagicine. The bandits are restrained and should give you no trouble, even that brute Samson, since it doesn't appear he can do any magic. Once I am done escorting her, I will return to Opulake and escort the rest of the bandits to Fort Mudo and meet you there."

Savant nodded slowly as he thought over Adonis's plan, and while he did, my heart seemed to stop beating.

"Okay, sure, that will work," he said finally. "Adonis, you will escort Odessa and Talicia home and make sure they arrive safely, and I will take Micah and

Arabella with me to Fort Mudo. Once you have returned her, meet us in Fort Mudo, we will wait for you there before returning to Jemny together."

Arabella? She would be going with the Mystio instead of me? We had become intimate friends in such a short time. I felt like I knew her better than some of the Pavrenis I had known my whole life.

Hurt welled up in me from the rejection, and I could tell Arabella felt it through our empathy link because she looked at me.

Adonis nodded his head at Savant's approval and looked at me.

"Pack quickly, eat if you need, and meet me downstairs at the base of the aid tower in an hour, we will leave immediately. I will get the plagicine and the horses ready."

Without waiting for an answer, he hurried out of the room and out of sight. Savant gripped my arm once again and gave me a piercing look.

"Once again, I thank you," he said. "You seem like a great warrior; we could always use your help in the Mystio Corp."

As I watched him walk away, I remembered something.

"Wait," I said, and Savant halted at the doorway. "In the arena, there's a copper Mystio badge. I used it to cut Samson. I don't have it here, so it may be there still. Maybe it's Eufaula's?"

Savant looked at me and nodded.

"Again, I am in your debt," he said and then he too left the room, leaving just Arabella, Talicia, and I alone in the room.

"So, you have got a little under an hour before you go home and finish your quest." Arabella smiled. "I know you guys are excited."

"Why aren't you coming with me?"

"Well, I have nothing here, my town is in shambles, my parents are gone, and my friend is dead. No, I do not need these memories here. I'm just following a feeling. I think I am needed with the Mystio until I can discover my new purpose."

She didn't mention her parents. Tripa Fons had said her parents were on a mission trip in Tyvent, which I knew was another country to the east. I didn't like that we were separating, but she was right, Pavrenes had nothing for her.

"What about the empathy link thing?"

Arabella stood up and placed her hand on my shoulder, and as she did, I felt Arabella's thoughts flow through my head like a cool and calm river.

Arabella smiled and removed her hand.

"You do not have to worry about me, Odessa," Arabella said. "We will see each other again. Let me know if you need anything, we have the empathy link. Take the plagicine and save your people. I am never farther than a thought away. Be safe."

With that, Arabella wrapped her arms around my neck and hugged me tightly. I hesitated and then hugged Arabella back.

We had just met, but I felt like she was a part of me, like my best friend, and I didn't want to leave her side, but she smiled at me, and I smiled back.

One new friend and one hundred new enemies.

Arabella then bent on one knee in front of Talicia, even though she was only an inch taller than the twelve-year-old, and hugged her.

"Be safe, Talicia, and protect your sister."

Arabella ran her hand through Talicia's already messy hair and somehow left it messier. Talicia smiled and shook her head.

Arabella waved once more and walked out of the room, but even as she did so, her presence still lingered in my mind. Our connection faded as she got farther away, but it never fully vanished.

This was the first time I'd been alone with Talicia in days. It was the first time our lives weren't in imminent danger. I sat down and pulled my little sister onto my lap, hugging her tightly.

"Are you okay?"

She nodded, continuing the hug.

"Don't we need to get ready?" she asked, burying her face in my chest.

"We've got an hour, and I decided we could sit for five minutes without the world ending," I replied. "I didn't know I was going to beat Samson and find you. If it wasn't for Arabella and what she taught me in the arena, we would all be dead probably."

Talicia laughed slightly and held up her hand in front of me. I gasped as she manifested a very thin layer of orange magic.

"Yeah, she is a good teacher."

Chapter SEVEN

eufaula

When your only possessions are the clothes on your back, it doesn't take long to pack.

Talicia and I searched the tower for new clothes. We managed to find some black pants close to our size and long sleeve shirts that kept the winter wind at bay. The shirt on me was purple while Talicia's shirt was blue instead.

I did find some light brown boots in my size, and I slipped them on and tucked my pants into the boots as the Mystio did. The boots looked brand new and besides my sword, they were now the fanciest things I owned.

Unfortunately, there was no footwear in Talicia's size, so she continued wearing the shoes she'd left Pavrenes in.

Once dressed, Talicia led me to the kitchen where we ate stale biscuits and drank tea that tasted like a mixture of peach and strawberries. I wish we had more of Jacob's bread to go with it, but it had gone down with the *Estonia*.

I was beginning to feel better about our situation. Samson had been defeated and detained by the Mystio, Talicia and I had been reunited, relatively unhurt, and we had been delivered an actual cure.

The plagicine was more than I had hoped for. Adonis was even going to make sure we got to Pavrenes safely with the cure. With him there, we wouldn't have to worry about the First Constellation interfering.

I had heard of few things that could defeat a Mystio in a fight, yet Samson had. I shivered at the thought of stronger bandits in the First Constellation. I just hoped we would make it back in time to save Grimke and the rest of the sick Pavrenis.

The only thing we valued that was missing was our weapons, so we spent the remainder of our time searching the tower, village, and the arena. In the arena, I also searched for the Mystio badge, but it wasn't there. Either it had been stolen by the pirates or Savant had already retrieved it.

We returned to the aid tower empty-handed and stood at the base, waiting for Adonis to meet us.

"Where did you get that cool dagger?" I asked Talicia.

"It's Dad's," she replied, staring at the ground. "I took it out of his room when we left. I figured, you know, it would be mine when I got older, like your sword. But now it's gone. I hope he won't be mad when he wakes up."

Her voice was tinged with sadness, and she stared at the ground absently. I knew how she felt, I had lost my sword and scabbard. Like my sword, if Grimke died, the dagger would have been the last thing she could claim of his.

It made sense that she had got it from Grimke's room, but what didn't make sense was Grimke possessing it. Where had he gotten such extravagant weapons?

"I'm sure he won't be too upset," I assured her. "He'll be more focused on your safety."

Talicia didn't reply, so I decided to change the subject. I wanted to talk with her to make sure she was truly okay.

"I'm not sure I did the right thing bringing you here," I admitted.

Talicia punched me lightly on the shoulder and smiled.

"As if I would've let you leave me. You needed help, and we're sisters," she said, intertwining her fingers through mine.

As our allotted time ended, Adonis appeared with two horses. One of the horses was charcoal grey with a light grey mane, and the other was mahogany brown with a black mane. While the charcoal horse neighed and shifted restlessly beside Adonis, the brown one stood quiet and looked on, as Talicia and I approached him.

"Thank you for being on time," said Adonis, as he fed the grey horse a carrot. "We will leave in one moment. Come closer so I can introduce you both."

Talicia and I approached him, and he gestured to the horses. They each had a purple blanket hanging down their sides with a white swan on it.

"These are Mystio horses. The grey is male, and his name is Judo. He has saved my life more times than I can count. The brown one is a female, and her name is Achuka. She is an extra horse and not assigned to anyone on our squad. She is stubborn but will never give up on you."

"Achuka," I whispered, as I rubbed my hand softly against her side.

She ignored me, unlike Scout who always nuzzled against my touch. Talicia walked over to Judo and studied him. It was our first time seeing a horse of that color.

"Odessa, look," she said.

"Yeah, I know, it's a pretty color," I said. I was looking at the ruins of Opulake, hoping to see Arabella once more, even though we had already given our official goodbyes and I could barely feel her through the empathy link.

"No, look," Talicia insisted.

I turned and followed her gaze. Strapped to the side of Judo was my sword. I glanced at Adonis who was watching me closely. Had he known this was my sword? Or had he simply found it and claimed it for his own?

"That's my sword. The bandits stole it when they kidnapped us."

Without another word, Adonis strode over to where the sword was attached to Judo, unstrapped it, and gripped it tightly.

"This is Backstabber. It is a dwarven blade and was used to kill the last dwarven king, High King Potiphar. This was the High King's blade."

Adonis held the blade up and it glinted and seemed to glow slightly as if it was absorbing all the light around it. He studied it once more and then carefully handed it to me.

Backstabber? Was that the sword's true name? Is that why Grimke had kept it secret?

"How did you come by such a weapon? This is one of the few known black blades left."

"My father gave it to me. He is the man I'm trying to save. His name is Grimke."

Something flashed in Adonis's eyes. Even though he quickly covered it, I saw the surprise in his eyes. *Does he know my father?*

"Did you happen to find a dagger?" interrupted Talicia, as I mounted Achuka.

"What kind of dagger?" he asked, mounting Judo, "Was the blade black like Backstabber?"

"No, just a normal steel dagger, I think, with a red gem on the hilt, like a ruby."

"A red gem? No, I haven't seen any daggers like that."

I climbed onto Achuka and made myself comfortable before extending my arm towards Talicia below me.

Disappointed, Talicia grabbed my outstretched arm and mounted the horse. Once her arms were wrapped securely around my waist, I nodded to Adonis. We were ready.

The sheathe to my sword was missing, so I had to either hold the sword or tie it to the horse as Adonis had done on Judo. I decided to do the latter.

Adonis and Judo took off down the road east towards Astria and the fading Zaniah. I urged Achuka after Adonis. We had the cures. We were going home. The quest was nearly over.

○

We rode in silence, and despite my curiosity about the Mystio and what Adonis knew of magic, I opted to not ask.

After Astria and Zaniah had set completely, Adonis announced that we should camp for the night and rest.

Talicia had already fallen asleep as we rode. We were in the Montoya Forest, and it was a much different forest from the Queenslen Forest on the island.

It was the first time I'd traveled through it while conscious, and while the trees in the Queenslen Forest kept their leaves and flowers in the winter, most of the trees in the Montoya Forest were barren and empty.

Adonis found a small clearing not far from the road and began unloading his gear. The night was cold, so while he gathered wood, I tried to clear the snow so that we could lie more comfortably.

I shivered as Adonis stacked a pile of wood and almost instantly set the wood ablaze despite it probably being moist from the snow.

"Here, take this," Adonis said, handing me a rolled-up mat. "There should be another on Achuka. I usually need two."

"Thank you."

I gently shook Talicia awake, helped her dismount Achuka, and laid her on the mat. Then I grabbed the mat on the side of Achuka and rolled it out.

"Is there any food or water for the horses?"

"No, but they can graze on the grass," replied Adonis, with a shrug. "They'll be fine using the snow for water."

"Any food for us? I'm starving."

Adonis reached into a pouch attached to Judo and pulled out two apples, one red and one green, and tossed them to me. He then sat down on the log and dropped his head.

I caught the apples and laid the red one next to Talicia and decided to keep the green one for myself.

"Are these magic?" I asked as I studied the green apple closely.

"No, they're just apples," Adonis said. I thought I heard a smile in his voice, but when I looked at his face, it was bare of any humor.

I nodded my thanks and began munching on the apple. It was tart and tangy, but I loved the taste of green apples.

I sat down and stared at the fire. It flickered and glowed warmly. I wasn't very tired and would have much preferred to ride through the night.

We were racing against time. I had slept too long, and we needed to get to Pavrenes as soon as possible. Adonis was our escort and had decided to stop. I didn't voice my opinion and decided to trust his judgment, although I did consider riding onward without him.

I focused on my frustration and my aura appeared cloaking me in purple light. I raised my arms still in awe of the magic.

"I did hear from Savant that you could Channel. Level four, it looks like."

I looked up and saw him studying me. I thought he had dozed off along with Talicia, but his eyes were alert. His voice broke my concentration and my aura vanished.

"What do you know about the Elohan Faith Magic?" I asked.

"The Elohan Cult is more like it. They "channel" and believe that their faith allows them to use magic, but in reality, almost every person in this world can use some sort of magic, and Channeling is only one of them, and is by far the easiest to use."

Arabella had mentioned other kinds of magic when we were in the arena facing Samson. I recalled the Elohans, Channelers, and the Djinni. When I didn't speak, Adonis continued speaking.

"The dwarves taught humans how to Channel when they first came to this land long ago, and the dwarves themselves learned to Channel from the giants. Most humans are mundane creatures; they have no magic of their own, so they Channel their life energy as auras that can be used in numerous ways. It is the easiest form of magic and probably the most adaptable. That's why all Mystio and Rangers are taught how to Channel in basic training. Some people instead prefer to get their power from deities or through sacrifices. These kinds of magic are called Holy Magic and Death Magic."

"Where are the dwarves now?"

"After the dwarves taught the first humans magic, how to survive in this country, and how to have basic hygiene, they turned on the dwarves."

107

He paused and looked at me. *Was he judging me?*

"The dwarves were far more powerful; you see dwarves are born with magic themselves. They don't need to Channel magic, they *are* magic. But humans soon outnumbered the dwarves, and once it seemed the war was lost, they fled across the sea and to their underground cities."

"I've never heard any of this before," I said softly.

"You're a Pavreni, right? From the unnamed island? Not surprising."

Though his words hurt me, they were true. Pavrenes was far from a cultural hub, and besides Grimke, I had learned little history outside of the island's history, and that only went back about two hundred years.

"That island had a dwarven name once before. I don't know what it was, but dwarves weren't big fans of sailing, and so when the war started, they abandoned the island first and its name was lost. Some humans would start a colony and name it Pavrenes, but the island itself was never renamed. That's why it's still unnamed."

"How do you know so much about the dwarves?"

"My grandfather was a dwarf," he said, with pride. "His power is mine now. Dwarves have been hunted by the crown since the War of the White Swan ended. My father hid me, but- but eventually we were found. My father was killed trying to protect us, my mother was sent to jail, and I was conscripted."

His words shocked me. Many claimed that the Queen was a caring and noble ruler, even better than the King before his death.

Adonis stood up and his aura roared to life. It extended well over a foot from his body and was a dark purplish red, like wine. I could hear it, it hummed and chimed softly with life, and it made the clearing feel just a bit colder.

"The sword you have, Backstabber, you say you got it from your father. What is his full name?"

"Grimke of Pavrenes, he's the mayor there. Mayor Grimke, but we don't have a last name. We're nobodies."

"Nobody is a nobody," Adonis said, letting his aura die down.

"Why are you asking about my father?"

"My father's name was Numenor. He told me about a dwarf named Grimke. His sword was named Backstabber because he stabbed the Dwarvish King Potiphar in the back. Without a leader, the dwarvish clans fell into disarray and they were forced to flee. He is said to be the main reason the dwarves lost to the humans, but you may think it couldn't be the same Grimke because that was over a hundred years ago, yet, the dwarves live much longer than humans, and you have his blade in your possession."

"My father is no dwarf. He's human. He's even taller than you. And he would never kill anyone unless it was for self-defense."

109

Adonis scoffed harshly.

"Dwarves aren't short. They're about human height, maybe a bit shorter than humans on average, but they got the name "dwarf" from the giants, who were larger than the aid towers. They were the size of mountains. Even humans would be considered "dwarves" to the giants if they were still here today."

I fell silent, trying to wrap my head around this latest information.

"There is one way to know for certain whether your father is a dwarf or not."

He got up and began to walk toward me. I suddenly felt uneasy.

"How's that?" I asked hesitantly. I stood and took a step back from him.

"Dwarven genes are dominant over human genes. Even someone with a dwarven grandparent will have genes that are predominantly dwarven."

"Yes, but what's the test?"

"Dwarves have their own form of magic, you'll simply need to speak the words of power, and if you're dwarven, the magic will manifest, and if not, then it won't."

Another type of magic, it was getting hard to keep track of them. So, there was Elohan Faith Magic or Channeling, Death Magic, Holy Magic, and now Dwarven Magic.

Before we could continue, the air suddenly shifted. It was now much colder, as if we had been hit by a sudden cold front, and the wind began howling hysterically. Adonis paused and looked out at the fields in the distance.

"Banshee," he said, as he reached for his sword.

"Banshee?" I repeated.

I had no idea who or what that was, but as Adonis pulled out his sword, I mimicked him.

Our fire was snuffed out by a heavy gust of wind, and we were left only with the light of Ithil until a cloud blocked its light too and we were left in darkness.

Lighting up the shadows down the road, I could see something glowing and approaching us. Was it a spirit like the Pavrenis claimed haunted the Queenslen Forest?

I moved slowly and positioned myself between the spirit and Talicia, who was lying near the fire.

A low moan pierced the silence. It started as a moan, then a hum, and then a melody developed from the humming. Although the spirit said no words, the tune was one of melancholy.

It emitted a light pink aura, and once it drew nearer to us, the light shifted from a vague circular form and took the shape of a woman, and the hum changed its pitch.

Her notes were low, but I could hear her clearly despite the distance. It was weird, her song had no words, but I could somehow feel that her song was one of betrayal and misfortune.

As the light of Ithil returned, the banshee was illuminated, and I was shocked to see she was another Mystio, as she wore the same uniform I'd seen Savant and Adonis in, but there was no cape, and her uniform was damaged severely.

Her feet were bare, and her body hovered slightly off the ground. Her pants were torn with large patches of the fabric missing and her chest plate was shattered into two pieces, hanging loosely from the straps on each shoulder.

"What is a banshee?"

"Sometimes when a magically strong human dies before releasing their magic, the energy duplicates their spirit. It is quite rare, but the human dies and the magic unutilized looks to return to the body, but with the original soul gone, the magic is left behind. Usually, the magic fades, but other times, it reaches a state of homeostasis, and at that point, the magic is self-sufficient and no longer wasting away."

The banshee levitated higher until it floated over us, with her eyes fixed on us. She continued her song and appeared to listen to us as we spoke.

"How do we defeat a banshee?" I asked.

"That's the thing," Adonis said, keeping his eyes on the creature. "We don't. Banshees are too powerful and immune to physical attacks. We may be able to defeat her with magic, but I'm reluctant to fight if I don't have to. She may leave after her song. Stay calm. We don't want to startle her, or she may shriek. The shriek of a banshee is said to be an omen of death. Wherever they go, death follows."

"She's a Mystio too, do you know her?" I asked, after glancing at Talicia to make sure she was still safe.

"That is Eufaula."

"Savant's partner?" I whispered.

Adonis nodded.

"Yes, they are *inamorata*. It is similar to the empathy bond you share with Arabella, but deeper. It is the ultimate form of intimacy between two or more people in love. They become almost one, their thoughts and emotions fully open. When one dies, like with Eufaula and Savant, they don't always die together like the empathy link. But, when only one lover dies, the other suffers immense pain, and some even go insane. It's as though a part of their soul has died. Not all lovers participate in it, and it is a crazy ritual, but in exchange, the partners have seamless communication, increased intimacy, and perfect levels of empathy."

"Will Savant be okay?"

Adonis grimaced.

"He'll recover eventually, I'm sure. I've heard the hardest part is the initial shock and loss, but I do not have an *inamorata* myself, so I can't say for sure. What I can say is that I think we're currently in a worse position than he is right now."

Eufaula the Banshee continued to sing yet I did not understand the words she sung. She had a lovely voice and I wondered if that was what Eufaula sounded like in life or if becoming a banshee gave her a good singing voice.

"I wish there was a way to tell Savant she's here," I said.

"You could. You have an empathy bond with Arabella, and Arabella is with Savant, but telling him right now would not help. They're too far away right now and you need to focus on the situation. She could wail at any time, and if you're not ready, you could die. I'll report it to Savant when I see him next."

His words made Eufaula's song seem eerier, her eyes glazed over as she watched us, and it was at this point I decided to wake Talicia in case she needed to flee.

Talicia was slow to wake. She cleared the sleep from her eyes, and she saw the banshee floating over us. Her eyes widened and she yelped in panic.

"A ghost!" she said.

"Banshee," Adonis corrected, keeping his eyes on Eufaula.

Eufaula turned her focus on Talicia and her song faltered for a second.

"But if she's a banshee, doesn't that mean she's dead? How is she up there?" Talicia said, pointing directly at Eufaula.

114

I didn't know how Talicia knew about banshees when I, myself, didn't, but Eufaula did not like being called a ghost, or maybe it was Talicia calling her dead, because at Talicia's words, Eufaula stopped singing and the forest was dead silent.

"Here it comes," Adonis said, raising his sword and pointing it to the forest. "There's nothing else we can do. Run, cover your ears best you can, and focus."

I was tired of finding myself in "nothing else we can do" situations. I grabbed Talicia's hand tightly and pulled her up onto her feet as I followed Adonis's retreat.

The dark forest suddenly felt like all the air was being sucked out of it and I knew it had something to do with the banshee, but I was focused on Talicia and did not know how she was causing the shift in the environment.

"Go!" I yelled to Talicia, pushing her forward. I glanced back at the gear remaining on the ground. We would need the supplies if we were going to make it to Pavrenes alive.

Adonis was speaking quickly to the horses, and they quickly ran past Talicia who was running east down the road.

I decided not to risk it and took a single step after Talicia and Adonis. Eufaula's eyes flashed brighter, and she began to wail.

The wail penetrated deep into my ears. My feet remained planted on the ground, and I was frozen in place, unmoving, and a thousand years passed.

115

Chapter EIGHT

adonis

"I'm not mad, I'm just disappointed," my mother said.

She leaned against the doorway of our home, looking down at me. Her face was devoid of any emotion; there was no affection, no love.

I stood frozen, by Eufaula's wails, as memories of my mother filled my head. Eufaula glided towards me, her mouth wide open, as her hair stood up on its ends. My heart pounded, as I watched her drift closer, unable to escape her lament.

I could not even cover my ears and I was exposed to the full sound of her scream. It drilled deep into my head reaching into every nook and cranny of my mind.

Out of the corner of my eyes, I saw Adonis had freed the horses and was now running towards me. The closer he got to me and Eufaula's wails, the slower he moved. Luckily, and unluckily, Talicia was nowhere in sight.

Adonis had warned me that defeating a banshee was impossible. She drew closer and her song kept me ensnared while filling my mind with thoughts of my mother.

I couldn't even close my eyes to blink, so I focused on hers, as I tried Channeling my magic. Violet sparks popped throughout my body like miniature purple fireworks, but they disappeared just as quickly.

My magic couldn't save me this time. I was powerless.

As she inched closer, I studied her carefully. We were almost face to face at that point. The banshee's eyes looked over my frozen figure with what looked like curiosity. She was a beautiful woman, even as a banshee.

I could see why Savant would have liked her. She had large eyes and full lips that glowed with the pink aura emanating from her.

What did banshees want? Was she going to kill me? Eat me? And if so, what was she waiting on? Was she the type of monster to play with her food?

"Parlay," I said, lifting both arms wide open.

The words took a long time to leave my mouth and my hands took an eternity of waiting until they were fully raised while under the banshee's song.

"Eufaula O'Conner. That's your name, right?"

My thoughts were focused on memories of our home, with my mom still standing by the doorway and looking down at me.

Now, she strode closer and sat at the dining room table next to me. Although she was now at eye level, I continued to look at the floor to avoid her cool gaze.

"As the oldest, I expect you to set a better example. You cannot keep shirking your responsibilities and training, Odessa."

She cupped my chin with her hand and lifted my head gently and I was forced to look at her directly in her eyes.

We had the same hazel eyes and no one else in Pavrenes had the same eyes as us, but on my mother, the eyes looked like they were the eyes of a hunter and on me, they only looked like normal eyes.

"It's very important that you focus on these things."

I had heard the speech a couple of times before and I pulled my face out of her hand. I didn't reply but nodded my head quietly.

I had only fallen behind on my readings. It had not been a big deal. Besides, what did it matter that King Ambrocio had died due to too much water in his lungs or that some species of fish regrew teeth their whole lives and some even glowed in the dark?

I had never met the King and I would never encounter such deep ocean fish. I had never left the island and I could not swim.

I shook my head and tried expelling the memory from my mind. Now wasn't the time to reminisce about my mother. I needed to concentrate.

I slowly bit my lip, hoping the pain would help me focus. As my teeth dug into my bottom lip, I was able to focus on my surroundings once more, but little had changed.

Adonis and Eufaula were in almost identical positions to where they'd been previously, and Talicia, Achuka, and Judo were still hidden from my sight.

Before I could use my focus to think up a counteraction, the memories won the struggle, and soon they returned to my mind stronger than ever.

Was Eufaula responsible for this? Was the song bringing back these memories?

I could feel her presence in my mind, and if not for the empathy link with Arabella, I would not have known what it felt like, but it seemed like Eufaula was looking for something in my memories.

My memories shifted to a scene later that day. I was outside and Talicia was standing next to me, pouting. I saddled up Scout and ran my hand down his side with a smile. I closed the flaps of the saddlebags and glanced at the sky.

It was a warm and windy summer day on the island. Both Astria and Zaniah were at each of their peaks, and it was the perfect weather for riding.

"Aw, come on, Odessa! You said I could go riding with you today. I bet you're going with Mahalia the Second and Victorija too, but you won't take me? That's not fair."

I sighed and dropped to my knees, and placed my hands on her shoulders gently. She avoided my eyes, and she kicked the ground with her foot which caused a cloud of dirt to cloak her.

"Sorry, but I'll take you next time, I promise. Today, it's just me and-"

Colden.

The moment his name came into my thoughts, I was released from the memory. I stumbled back and grabbed my chest. Eufaula's wail transitioned back into her sad singing.

I was for a moment unfrozen, but I still had little control. Before I could move away from Eufaula, reality faded once more as an unfamiliar memory suddenly played in my mind.

It was Colden. He was laying down, with his hair standing on its ends. I had never seen his hair so short, and his face was smeared with something black and filth.

He lay motionless on his side and smiled up at me and his brown eyes did not blink.

He was dead.

This was not my memory.

Was it a vision? Was Colden in danger?

I looked into Eufaula's eyes. Adonis had said they were omens of death. Perhaps the banshees were not the actual causes of the death and just the messengers. If that was the case, her premonition gave me the chance to save Colden.

Thank you.

She stopped singing and levitated so close, we were almost cheek to cheek. Slowly, she took her hand and placed it on my breast, above my heart. Her pink aura left an outline on my chest, and slowly, she faded away.

Adonis stopped by my side, breathing loudly as he pointed to my chest and the spot where Eufaula had disappeared.

"What was that? What did she say?"

Drifting back to reality, I remembered the gravity of the situation. Beckoning him, I ran towards our gear and started gathering as much as I could carry.

"She didn't say anything, but she did warn me. Colden is in trouble, and we need to get to Pavrenes as soon as possible."

"We're already moving at the most efficient pace," he countered, grabbing the remaining gear. "These aren't ranger ponies. They can't go all day and all night. They need rest."

"We don't have time for rest," I insisted. "I need to find Talicia and we need to go now."

"Okay, wait," he said, stepping in front of me and holding his palm out. "The fastest way to get there may be to use whey and energy transfers. But, for a level four Channeler like you, it could be dangerous."

I opened my mouth to question him, but he interrupted me. I still did not know what a level four Channeler was.

"Let's find your sister first and then I'll explain it. I'm sure she's out there frightened and alone."

I nodded, and he turned to the forest and whistled loudly. A few seconds later, we heard hooves growing louder. Both horses appeared in the clearing, stopping beside Adonis.

"They don't go far," Adonis explained, as he saddled up the horses.

We both climbed on the horses and rode off in the direction Adonis said Talicia had taken off in. The forest was eerily silent. Finally, Adonis began to speak.

"Whey is an infused form of bread," he explained, slowing down to ride beside me. "It was developed in the capital and rationed out to some of the Mystio, Rangers, and soldiers. It's special because it can restore a person's energy. It helps them fight and Channel as if they were fully rested. But when it wears off, they're left feeling extremely exhausted. It can be addictive, and the built-up stress that hits your body and mind all at once can kill you or break your sanity."

"Sounds risky."

"It is," he said, studying me. "You have a strong spirit, but you barely know the basics of Channeling, so there's a chance your body will die on you."

Our conversation was interrupted, as we came around a curve in the road and spotted a woman balled up on the ground, crying.

Adonis issued a whistle and both Achuka and Judo halted. While Adonis pulled out his sword, I dismounted Achuka unarmed and approached the woman in the road.

"Help," the woman cried, stretching out a bloodied hand in our direction. "Please help."

I knew everyone from Pavrenes, and she wasn't one of us. We were so close to Pavrenes that I couldn't imagine her being from anywhere else as we were on the very edge of the kingdom.

There was nothing on this side of the kingdom besides the destroyed Opulake and the sick Pavrenes. Perhaps she was another member of the First Constellation.

"Odessa, wait," Adonis warned as I made my way toward the woman.

We needed to find Talicia, but I knew if we rode past the hurt woman without aiding her, Grimke would be disappointed, as would Colden. I needed to help her first. I manifested my aura and continued to approach her.

"Are you okay?" I asked, kneeling beside her.

Before I could react, the woman grabbed my hand, and I yelped, surprised by her strong grip. She sneered up at me, as the trees behind her rustled.

"Odessa," Adonis said evenly. There was something off about how he said my name, so I looked at him and followed his eyes to see what he was looking at behind me.

I saw the three men standing behind her with rusty jagged swords and axes. They wore black, the uniform of the First Constellation, all black, and red stars.

How many of these criminals are there? I wondered.

"Give us those horses and everything you've got, and I'll let her go," the woman snarled at Adonis.

Her words were similar to Olympia's, and I wondered if all the bandits got the same script for robberies.

This lady was nowhere near as big and strong as Samson. I was ready to fight and took a deep breath to prepare myself and wait for Adonis's signal, but instead of stabbing or charging, he sheathed his sword and held his hands up in surrender.

"Adonis, what are you doing?" I demanded to know.

"Stay still," he commanded, keeping his eyes on the bandits.

The bandits cackled as they walked forward.

"Fussiladi," Adonis said in a voice so low it was almost a whisper.

Three blasts of blazing red fire burst out of his hand and hit each pirate square in the chest. Their faces remained frozen in shock as each fell with a loud thud to the ground. The woman squeezed my hand tighter, and I cried out in pain.

Adonis turned his glare towards her.

"Let her go," he ordered, as the purple aura radiated from his hand. "Or you're next."

The woman's anger quickly turned to fear as she dropped my hand and crawled to his feet, begging for her life.

I got up from the ground and dusted myself off, staring at the pitiful figure in disgust. I started walking towards Achuka, but stopped when I realized Adonis wasn't following me. He stepped closer to the wailing woman.

"Where are you from, mercenary?" he barked.

The woman didn't answer, but her wails got louder. The sound echoed in the dark and dreary forest.

"I don't have time for a prolonged interrogation. Tell me who hired you and where you're from and I'll let you go.

The woman stopped her weeping.

"We are mercenaries from the Green Lion Guild of Cypress. We were hired by Lord Cicero in Umbar and are working with the First Constellation to capture this part of Damasyr."

They were two countries that bordered Damasyr in the south. I knew little about Umbar, and even less about Cypress.

What were they doing here?

"What were you specifically hired to do?" Adonis asked.

Something flickered in a tree nearby. *Talicia?* I turned to investigate, but before I could react, a bolt of fire pierced through the air and hit the woman on her chest. The woman screamed as her body burst into flames.

"Adonis," I cried, running towards him.

He turned, grabbed my hand, and ran towards the horses.

"It's Dwarven Magic!" he yelled. "Look," he said, pointing up at a tree branch and I saw a cloaked figure turning and jumping to the next tree branch down the road away from us.

I climbed Achuka and raced towards the fleeing figure that jumped nimbly from branch to branch. They were fast, but I was gaining on them. Adonis and Judo were behind, racing to catch up.

I dug my hand into Achuka's saddlebags, looking for rope or a grappling hook, but all I found was a rusty crossbow. I aimed it at the attacker, but between Achuka's gallop and the stranger's jumping, I couldn't get a solid shot. I fired anyway and missed.

Frustrated, I shoved the crossbow back into the bag and tried Channeling my aura. The retreating figure had used the same fire magic as Adonis. He'd called it Dwarven Magic, and earlier, he implied that I may have been dwarven too. If I were, that would mean that I had the same magic as them.

What was the word Adonis had muttered? Fussiladi?

I raised my left hand and aimed my palm at the retreating figure the best I could and inhaled and exhaled quickly.

Here goes nothing.

"*Fussiladi*!" I shouted.

My body vibrated as the words passed my lip, and my hands burned as a sudden bolt of purple light erupted from my palm. My purple bolt hit its mark. The figure's dark green cape burst into flames.

The figure shrugged off the cape quickly and threw it to the ground. A long mane of red hair emerged as the cape fell and was quickly extinguished by the snow when it hit the ground.

"It's a girl," I yelled back to Adonis.

He yelled something back but was too far for me to make out his words. My palm was raw and throbbed harshly from the burst of fire, but I ignored it and aimed at the retreating figure again.

"*Fussiladi!*"

This time, the bolt of energy hit the branch of the tree she was about to land on. Without anywhere to land, she cried out and scrambled to grab any other branches, but she was unsuccessful as she fell to the snow-covered ground.

My hand erupted with an even stronger burst of pain, and I moaned at the feeling.

This magic sucks, I thought, as the throbbing continued. I hopped off Achuka and grabbed my sword with my right hand, as my left could not grip it properly because of the magic.

I dropped to the ground and buried my hand in the snow, hoping that the cold would cool the burning. I kept my sword ready, and with my aura activated, the gem on the blade's hilt appeared to glow slightly.

"Stay here," I told Achuka. Once my hand had improved as much as it could from the snow, and began cautiously approaching the girl on the ground.

As I stood over her and bent down to get a closer look, I glanced back to see where Adonis was, and that was when the girl flipped over quickly, kicked out her leg, and pulled my body from under me.

I lost my balance and fell to the ground, in a pile of snow. As the figure sat up, I realized she was a young girl, closer to Talicia's age than mine. She was dressed in expensive clothing that was vibrantly colored in oranges and reds. She was shorter than Talicia, with long red hair and reddish-brown eyes.

She threw two throwing knives at me, and with my left hand injured, I could only defend myself with my right. I blocked one knife but the other slashed my cheek.

Adonis arrived moments later.

"Talicia!"

My anger and pain melted away when I spotted my sister riding with Adonis and Judo. I got up and stumbled towards her, pulling her into me, as Adonis made his way towards the girl.

"Hello there, assassin," he said, coolly.

Keeping Talicia at my side, I turned around, just as the assassin threw three more knives at him, in an elegant arc. One missed, but the other two flew straight at him.

Adonis remained unflinching, as his aura flared to life and deflected both knives. He raised his hand, and the aura cloaked the girl, lifting her in the air and slamming her to the ground.

129

"Adonis." I gasped, while Talicia whimpered.

Adonis ignored me and kept his focus on the girl who appeared to be restrained by Adonis's aura as she struggled to move.

"You're no match for me," he told her, as he loomed above her crumpled figure. "Cooperate and I'll let you live."

I grabbed Talicia's arm and secured her on Achuka before making my way toward Adonis.

"What are you doing?" I argued, stopping beside him, and looking down at the girl.

"It's my duty to bring her to Jemny."

"What? You're supposed to come with us to Pavrenes."

He finally looked away from the girl and up at me. His face was emotionless, like a soldier in battle.

"I'll leave the cure with you, but this is the Sovereign's top priority. Alien fighters infiltrating our border should be immediately escorted and I'll have to take her with me. We are close to the Eastern Aid Tower and Pavrenes, so you should have no more trouble reaching the island and delivering the cures."

"What about its citizens, what does the *sovereign* care of that?" I asked.

Adonis scoffed. "The Queen-"

"Guys, look!" Talicia interrupted.

Talicia was pointing at the girl. Adonis's aura was becoming tainted as a beige aura was overriding the bordeaux color.

"Get back," yelled Adonis, grabbing my arm and pulling me back. He let out a two-tone whistle and the horses ran off with Talicia.

"What's going on?" I asked, as the beige energy slowly expanded.

"She's trying to blow herself up by converting her life energy into an explosion. She'll die, and if she does, we'll lose any intel we could've gotten from her."

Adonis raised his hands and aimed them at the girl. Two streams of bordeaux aura broke free and covered the spots of beige. It worked for a moment until more beige energy appeared in other spots.

The snow was beginning to melt around her, and the girl's eyes were now closed as steam rose from her body.

She's just a kid. I need to save her.

I focused and activated my aura. Placing my hands on Adonis's shoulder, I Channeled my energy through him, ignoring the pain in my left hand. As our auras intermixed, it slowly overpowered the beige energy.

But the process was slow, and I quickly became drained. With the beige energy almost restrained, I stumbled, losing my grip, and fell to my knees.

I tried producing more magic, but I was spent. I remembered the link I shared with Arabella and wondered if she would be able to help me with this but before I could attempt to reach out to her with my mind, Adonis spoke.

"Odessa," he groaned.

Adonis was still holding out his palms, though they were now visibly shaking, and his forehead was drenched with sweat. The purple aura was slowly disappearing, as the beige magic quickly overpowered my purple magic.

With one last shout, he forced a large burst of magic out of his hands and towards the girl. It contained the girl, and the beige began disappearing once again until the bordeaux aura stopped suddenly.

Adonis's arms hung at his sides limply and it appeared he was out of magic too. We had failed.

The beige energy cloaked the girl's body completely with no trace of our magic and we both watched in horror as her body shimmered and began to take on a ghostly form, like the one Eufaula the Banshee had taken.

I got up off my knees and attempted to pull Adonis back, who stood frozen, but he didn't budge, and I didn't have the energy to carry him.

I took a step back, and at that moment, the girl's beige aura exploded with a force that sent me flying into the sky. My head was knocked against something hard, and a second later, everything went dark.

Chapter NINE

sorbet

I moaned and clutched my head as I opened my eyes. My head pounded relentlessly and with each second it felt as if someone was using my head as a drum. I gingerly touched the tender spot on my head and winced at the contact.

The hair was sticky and dripping with blood.

I groaned as I moved slowly, and I was glad I did as I found myself high in one of the trees of the Montoya Forest and a sudden movement could have sent me falling to my death.

"Adonis?" I whispered, looking around the forest.

The young girl was gone, with only a black outline of her body scorched into the ground. The snow had melted from the explosion, and Adonis was lying unconscious in a puddle of water.

Grabbing onto one of the lower branches, I started my slow descent. The smell of burning flesh wafted through the trees, making me queasy.

With my left hand still burning from using the Dwarven Magic, I used my right arm to grip the branches, as I stepped downwards.

However, when I placed both feet on what I thought was a sturdy branch, it broke, and I started falling.

Instinctively, I reached out for a branch using my left arm and grabbed on, but the pain was too much. With a yelp, I let go and felt myself freefalling to the ground.

Bordeaux energy cloaked me and slowed my fall, but it shattered several feet off the ground, and I was dropped onto the ground. The impact hurt my back but at least I was alive, thanks to Adonis.

I turned to face him and saw he was still lying on the forest floor with one arm outstretched slightly. I dragged myself towards him quickly and studied him for blood and injuries.

"Are you okay?"

"Can't move," he grunted. "You whistle?"

"No, why?"

"Need horses, need whey," he groaned.

I pulled myself up to my knees, trying somewhat unsuccessfully to ignore the pain radiating through my entire body. Then I turned to Adonis and helped him up.

Adonis whistled weakly. The sound barely made it past the clearing. He stopped and leaned heavily against my shoulder as he caught his breath. I closed my eyes and fought the urge to collapse, as I held us both up.

Adonis whistled again. This time it was much louder. Moments later, we heard the horses approaching. I dragged us to the nearest tree and we both dropped down, leaning against the trunk of the tree as we tried to catch our breath.

"Bring your arms above your head, it'll help," he advised, as he did so himself.

I did as he suggested but I felt no difference. The horses appeared, trotting towards us with Talicia still on Achuka. Judo trotted over to Adonis while Talicia hopped off Achuka and ran toward me. She wrapped her arms around me and pulled me in. Pain erupted throughout my body, but I didn't want her to let go.

"Are you okay?"

She looked up at me, her cheeks wet with tears.

"I was so scared, I heard the explosion, but you told me to stay on the horse, so I did."

"So *now* you listen to me?" I asked, smiling weakly.

She laughed, loosening her grip as I ran my fingers gently through her hair.

"Well, hey, don't get used to it. I might not next time."

"Hopefully, there is no next time."

Zaniah was beginning its ascent on the horizon. Time was running out. Adonis grabbed Judo's saddle and lifted himself. Leaning against the horse, he rummaged through the saddlebag.

"Here," he said, tossing a tiny parcel at me. "It's whey. Unwrap it and take a small bite at first; a very small bite."

Adonis, who was currently munching on his own serving of whey, already looked like he was feeling better. I studied the parcel closely and saw that it was wrapped in a jet-black leaf.

Slowly, I unwrapped it and examined the contents within. It looked like a cross between bread and a cookie and was in the shape of a triangle.

I held it close to my nose and inhaled. It smelled like fruit. Cautiously, I took a small bite.

The moment it touched my tongue, I instantly felt better. It tasted like the lemon cream pie my mom would bake. I took another bite, and then another until I'd devoured the entire cookie. Stuffing the wrapper in my pocket, I got up and walked towards Adonis, who was busy readying the horses.

My left hand still felt raw, and the bruises along with the cut on my cheek were still there, but I felt energized and was able to move freely once again.

"This stuff is amazing," I said, stopping beside Adonis.

"Don't get used to it," he warned, looking at me as he secured our gear. "Emergencies only. We're lucky you survived the first time, considering you ate the whole thing. But you do have blood that's stronger than normal humans. You're something else, one of a kind for sure."

It sounded like a compliment, but his tone didn't match his words.

Was he talking about Grimke? Were there secrets that I didn't know?

"Do you have any cloth I can wrap this in?" I asked him, holding up my injured left hand.

He glanced at my hand, seemingly lost in thought as he straightened up and took a step closer.

"May I?" he asked, holding out his hand for mine.

I nodded, placing my hand gingerly into his open palms. He clasped both hands over mine, as a glow of bordeaux aura cloaked them. I winced, waiting for the pain, but it never came. Instead, it felt like thousands of ants were crawling inside my hand.

"Does all dwarven magic leave such great side effects?" I asked, thinking about the raw pain I felt when I shot the aura out of them.

"Only for the untrained," he said. "Hold still."

"So, Channeling can be used to heal too?"

"Yes, but it's rarely worth it to heal yourself unless you are on the verge of death, and at that point, you're probably dead anyways. If there's no hope, you might as well try. You use energy to heal, and by expending it, you will physically be better, but your magic will be reduced. Doing this enough can take a toll on your body and healing isn't going to work on large injuries unless you have large magic reserves and great skill. I'm going to leave your cheek unhealed, it's not as bad now, and we need our energy. We can still bandage it, though."

I nodded, watching the energy cloaking our hands.

"How are you doing this?"

"I am Channeling my aura with healing intent, commanding to heal, and then transferring energy to your hand. It's easy once you know how to manipulate your aura. It's similar to the energy transfer I mentioned previously. I manifest my aura, cloak the injured area, and use a healing intent."

Slowly, his aura died down and he released my hand. I examined it in awe, twitching my fingers and rotating my wrist. It was fully healed.

"Wow," I said, looking from my hand to him.

I gestured to the sore spot on the back of my head, and he inspected it. After wincing, he applied his healing magic to it and the heavy throbbing was reduced to a light thud.

Adonis reached into Judo's saddle and removed a single bandage. He quickly placed it over the cut on my cheek and then began mounting Judo.

I stood there for a moment and thought about how amazing magic was. I would have stood longer if not for Adonis who interrupted my thoughts by speaking.

"Come on, aren't we in a hurry?" he said looking down at me. He brought Judo in front of Achuka in preparation to depart.

I climbed onto Achuka, before reaching out and pulling Talicia up.

"So, you're not leaving us?" Talicia asked Adonis as she wrapped her arms around my waist and leaned forward on my back.

Adonis turned to the scorch marks on the road and shook his head.

"No point now, but we should proceed with caution. I could return and make a report, but that would be a waste. I will just have you reach out to Arabella, and you can have her relay the information to Savant. We should arrive at the Eastern Aid Tower today and with any luck, Pavrenes tonight or tomorrow. Plus, I want to meet this Grimke you speak of."

Today was the start of day nine since I'd departed. I was supposed to have been back yesterday. Colden would be worried sick. I could only hope Grimke was okay.

I tapped Achuka with my foot, but instead of trotting off, she trampled the mud in front of us.

"What's up with you?" I asked, climbing down to investigate.

Something gleamed in the mud. I bent down and grabbed the object. Turning it over, I saw faint markings on one side. I used the sleeve of my shirt and scuffed it clean.

'Sorbet Garcia: 1st Division'.

"Her name was Sorbet Garcia," I said, holding it out to show Adonis.

"It doesn't matter, let's go."

"Wait," I said, running towards him. "What do you mean it doesn't matter? She's dead. She was just a kid. She's dead because of us, because of me. Doesn't that mean anything to you?"

Adonis's expression remained unchanged as he looked down at me.

"We don't have time for this, Odessa. She was from an enemy country. Yes, she was young, but she made her choice. It was out of our control, we did our best to save her, but we shouldn't stay here. We've been in one position way too long as it stands. She was a soldier, and soldiers die. I won't mourn someone who would not do the same for me and neither should you."

Without waiting any further, he tapped Judo with his foot, and they were off. Talicia remained quiet on

Achuka, watching Adonis's departing figure. Sorbet was around her age. That could've been my sister.

I wiped the tears that had drifted down my cheeks and climbed back onto Achuka. Moments later, we were off.

My thoughts were only on Sorbet Garcia.

o

We rode in silence for hours.

Even though I had many questions, after our last conversation, I opted to remain silent.

The younger sun, Astria, was at its peak, shining down on us. The heat was a warm welcome, after the wintry night we'd endured. I thought about Arabella. I wondered if her journey with Savant and Micah was going better than ours.

This was the perfect time to test our empathy link. I took a breath and extended my mind.

Arabella?

I waited. Moments later, I felt her presence in my conscience.

Odessa. How is your journey going?

Her words felt like a familiar cool wave. It was comforting.

I'd had my doubts about us being able to converse. It just seemed like it would be impossible, with

141

us being so far away. But I could hear her and feel her. It was amazing. Magic was amazing.

I filled her in on everything that had happened; our run-in with Eufaula, the bandits, what Adonis wanted me to relay, and finally Sorbet's death.

Wow, are you okay? How far are you from Pavrenes?

I'm fine now, the whey got me in top shape, and he healed my hand. Adonis says we should get there by tonight or tomorrow.

You are so close. Stay smart. I will let Savant know what you have told me when I can. Let me know if you need anything, okay?

Although I wanted to talk more, I could tell that she was preoccupied. I wondered about her travels to Fort Mudo and hoped she was faring well.

My thoughts then shifted to Colden. I tried not to let Eufaula's vision get to me. I hoped he was safe. I knew he was worried about me. I was late and I was never late for anything.

I missed his presence. I always felt safe and warm in his hands. I just wanted to tease him about his long hair and how I hoped he didn't expect to have two wives like his father.

I needed his lips on mine. I wanted him to take me once more on the island beach. I felt foolish for having such thoughts at a time like now. I steeled myself for the task at hand.

We were almost there. I'd see him tomorrow at the latest. And despite all that Talicia and I had suffered, we were returning to Pavrenes victorious. We had the cure.

If Grimke had made this journey, there were a thousand ways he could've done it better. He wouldn't have let the *Estonia* sink and he could have beaten Samson by himself. He wouldn't have let Sorbet Garcia die. Would he have brought Talicia with him on the quest? Would he have brought me?

Both Astria and Zaniah were up in the sky now and the wind was blowing westward. There was a breeze as we rode, and it felt wonderful on my face.

I deeply breathed in the smell of the forest. After being stuffed in a cell, it was nice to be surrounded by trees, even if they did not still have their leaves.

I put one hand on Talicia's, which was still wrapped around my waist, and gripped it tightly. She squeezed mine back reassuringly.

"You know I love you, right?"

"I know."

We rode for another hour, with Talicia leaning against my back, fast asleep.

My faith in our quest was mending. After all, once we reached the Eastern Aid Tower, Pavrenes was less than a day away.

We just needed to find a boat or make a raft of some kind.

"Look," Adonis finally said.

I followed his gaze and saw the top of the Eastern Aid Tower in the distance. We were so close.

I smiled and quickened Achuka's trot.

"Stay alert," Adonis warned. "The air smells of battle."

As we got closer to the Eastern Aid Tower, I noticed the wisps of smoke rising from the tower and fading into the sky. *What happened to the tower? Had there been a pirate attack?*

About a mile away from the Eastern Aid Tower, Adonis made us get off the horses. He told the horses to wait until the next morning and then head to Fort Mudo. Before we left, he wrote something and then put a note into each of the horses' saddles.

I rubbed Achuka's snout fondly, told her goodbye, and gave her my thanks. Grabbing the bag from Achuka's saddle, I wrapped the plagicine vials carefully, before storing them in the bag and slinging it onto my back.

We crept towards the Eastern Aid Tower at a snail's pace. It was frustrating, but Adonis's orders had kept us safe so far.

He refused to enter another situation without having all the details.

As we got closer, we dropped down and crawled through the snow, mud, and dirt. We made our way to the base of the tower, which showed signs of a recent battle.

The large wooden door to the aid tower hung on its hinges, and several fallen bodies lay scattered on the shore, leading towards the beach in the direction of the island. None of the bodies moved and the beach was quiet except for the sound of the waves rushing up the shore.

As I stepped closer, I made a grim discovery. The bodies were Pavrenis. I ran past Adonis and towards the fallen bodies, checking and praying for signs of life. But the further I checked, the more hopeless I felt.

"Adonis," I started, turning to him with a tearful gaze.

At that moment, a cough interrupted us.

"Someone's alive," Talicia said and pointed towards the shore.

I looked towards the figure and Adonis asked, "Do you recognize him?"

Of course, I did. I would recognize him anywhere.

It was the butcher, Jacob.

145

Chapter TEN

jacob

"Odessa," Adonis said, looking at our surroundings cautiously. "We have to be careful here; this is the perfect place for an ambush. They may have left him there alive, as a trap."

I tried to focus my hearing but the only sounds I heard were the crashing of the waves and the creaking of the broken aid tower door, moving with the wind.

Maybe it was Adonis's words getting to me because I *did* feel as though there were eyes on us, watching our every move, but I saw no signs of life, human or otherwise, besides Jacob and the rest of the dead on the beach.

I'm just being paranoid, I thought, shaking my head, and focusing on Jacob.

"This is Colden's dad," I told Adonis. "I have to help him. I'm not asking. I'm going."

"Is he okay?" Talicia asked as she knelt beside me. "I can't really see from here. Can I come with you?"

I didn't want her to see him like this, but it may have been the last time she would see him alive if my medical knowledge and my magic failed us, so I nodded my head, and together we began to approach Jacob's body with Adonis following at a tactical distance.

Colden had often told me about his medical studies with his mother Reyna, but I rarely fully comprehended what he was explaining.

Once again I wished he were here. He would know what to do, and even if he didn't, he would get to see his father before he passed if we failed. He had taught me the basics of first aid, but the closer I got to Jacob's body, the more it looked like a hopeless enterprise.

Jacob looked rough. His eyes were closed, and his face was covered with battle scars, but luckily, he was still breathing. His right eye was swollen shut and there was a tuff of his hair missing in the front near his forehead.

It seemed completely unfair that he and the dead Pavrenis around him had survived the plague just to be sentenced to death by lawless bandits.

Adonis drew his sword and defensively circled us. He kept his eyes on our surroundings, while Talicia and I tended Jacob.

"This battle is fresh. We have no idea if enemies are waiting to attack. The man looks like he's wounded beyond help."

The man was a soldier. I guess it was too much to ask for empathy. I wondered if it was *his* father would he call it quits on him so quickly?

I let out a frustrated sigh and began rummaging through my bag in a desperate hope that I'd find something that could aid him. When that proved unsuccessful, I turned to Adonis.

"What about aura healing? Or the energy transfer you mentioned?"

Adonis glanced away from his patrol briefly to shake his head at me.

"That works for small and medium injuries. This man looks mortally injured, and his aura is almost empty. I can feel it. Even if you put all your energy into him, he may still die, and you along with him. Energy transfers allow you to transfer energy from one being to another but giving him energy won't help him if his body is already dying."

"What about the whey?"

Adonis shook his head once more.

"You've already had it once today. Two in one day can be extremely dangerous. Is it worth trading your life for his? Remember also that your life is tied to Arabella's and that if you die and your father dies, there is no one left to watch your sister. I don't mean to get involved and it's none of my business, but I have heard your story. You've worked very hard to get here and you should think hard about this decision because it could reverse everything you've done since you left home."

I glared up at Adonis, as Talicia looked from him to me, defeated.

"What about an empathy link?"

Adonis sighed, shaking his head as though I was a petulant toddler.

"Those work with magic exhaustion, not physical damage like this. And you already have an empathy link. Jacob would have to bond with you and Arabella, and Arabella isn't here. I know you're new to magic, but we should never depend on it. There are also circumstances where things like death are indomitable, and no form of magic can beat it."

Jacob coughed, and his chest rattled. I placed my head on his chest and listened carefully. His breathing was strained.

"What about Death Magic?"

"Forbidden. I couldn't teach it to you even if I knew how to."

I looked at Talicia's tearful face and back at Jacob. If it were her, I'd try everything in my power to save her life, even if it killed me. I needed to do the same for Colden's father.

Closing my eyes, I focused and conjured my aura. Once my hand was covered in the purple energy, I

Channeled my healing intent into him as I placed my hand on his chest.

My aura traveled across his body, illuminating him in a purple glow. It was fantastical to watch as the gash on his forehead knitted itself up.

He groaned, opening his eyes slightly.

"Odessa?" he croaked.

"Shhh," I whispered, holding my focus as the swelling around his right eye went down.

I put a large chunk of my magic into his chest and commanded it to heal. Once I was satisfied I raised my hands off his body. I felt drained but seeing Jacob sitting up and dusting himself off in awe was worth it.

"Colden and Tanner," he coughed.

"Where are they?" I asked, worried.

Adonis, who was finally satisfied that no enemy was about to attack us, stepped closer so that he could hear Jacob's strained words.

"We were split up in the attack," he said, turning his head towards the island.

"Attack? What attack, Jacob?"

Adonis passed a flask of water to me, and I carefully poured it into his mouth. Once it was empty, I wiped his mouth. Jacob looked at me with worry etched on the lines of his face.

Odessa and the First Constellation

"The First Constellation bandits arrived on the island shortly after you left. They demanded supplies, and when we refused, they killed Gianni, burned down the forge, and took most of the weapons from the armory."

Gianni was the blacksmith of Pavrenes. He could make anything out of metal and his death hurt a lot. And now I was losing Jacob. What could I do?

"They'll pay for this," I said, looking at the ocean. "Where could Colden and Tanner be?"

Jacob sighed, looking at the ocean. He then turned his gaze curiously to me and then to Adonis, before settling on the horses with their saddlebags.

"Did you- did you bring back the tonics?"

"Yes, I've got a bunch in my bag."

I got up and walked to the bags, taking one of the vials out. As I walked back to Jacob, I saw that he was lying on the sand once again, with Talicia bent over him.

"Jacob," I said, running over and dropping down beside him. "Are you okay?"

"Let me see it," he whispered.

Quickly, I pulled a plagicine out of my bag and gently placed it in his hands.

He turned it over, examining the vial as the tears flowed from his eyes.

"Tell my boys and my wives that I love them. Please."

151

With those final words, he closed his eyes and didn't move anymore.

"No, no, no," I cried, looking down at him. Talicia whimpered, and I felt Adonis kneeling beside me. I didn't know why he would bother now.

I need to save him. If I exhaust myself, Adonis will give me the whey. He wouldn't let me die, just as I wouldn't let Jacob die.

I focused my aura and placed my hands on Jacob's chest. This time, I Channeled my healing intent with as much energy as I could muster. My reserves were low, but minutes later, all of Jacob's wounds were healed.

I sat and waited for him to open his eyes.

"Jacob?"

His eyes remained shut. I placed my head on his chest and listened. My body shook when I realized that I was met with silence. There was no heartbeat.

Adonis placed his hand on my shoulder, as Talicia and I mourned the loss of a man we loved like a second father. After all the tears were spent and silence befell the shore, Adonis got up and held his hand out.

"We should get moving. Let's check the tower and then make our way towards the island."

I contemplated mentioning my vision from Eufaula to Adonis. There hadn't been the time before, but I didn't want to talk at that moment.

When I didn't speak or accept his hand, Adonis silently walked away toward the entrance of the Eastern Aid Tower. Talicia and I watched him walk away and held onto each other.

"Are you ready?" I asked, giving her a tight squeeze. I wished we could have sat there and mourned, but Grimke was so close, and every second was vital.

Talicia nodded, so I stood up and wiped the sand off my body. I helped my sister up and did the same for her. After looking at Jacob's body once more, we both walked towards the tower after Adonis.

Many of the fallen bodies were familiar faces.

There was Virginia, one of the tavern servers.

Volo.

Baluga.

Joel.

Our somber walk was interrupted when we heard the clashing of swords. I pulled Talicia behind me and pulled out my sword, stepping closer to the tower. As we made our way through the entrance and into the dark tower, I spotted Adonis in combat with a First Constellation bandit.

Adonis and the enemy jabbed and parried each other skillfully. I held up my sword and made my way toward them, but I was exhausted after using so much magic on Jacob.

Adonis stabbed the man in the thigh, and he stumbled back. Taking advantage of the moment, Adonis pressed forward, but the man quickly regained his composure and landed two quick slashes, hitting Adonis just below his Mystio chest plate on his stomach.

As the wound began bleeding, Adonis pressed his right hand on it to slow the bleeding, and defended himself as the man pressed him.

"Odessa, we have to help," Talicia said, pulling my sleeve.

"Stay here."

Mustering what little strength remained, I ran to Adonis's side and slashed my blade at the swordsman. He blocked my blow easily, but it gave Adonis just enough time to swing his blade at the man's neck. The man dropped to the floor.

I wanted nothing more than to step forward and interrogate the fallen man. *Was he responsible for Jacob's death? Was he the evil being that wreaked havoc on Pavrenes?* But Adonis was wounded and needed me more. The interrogation would have to wait.

"Here, take this," Adonis said, handing me a parcel of whey, "And then heal me."

I ate it immediately and felt the power surge through my body. I felt refreshed and at the top of my game, yet my sorrow held me down. Once every piece was gone, I summoned my aura and focused it on Adonis's stomach.

154

When Adonis was completely healed, we both cautiously searched the rest of the tower. There were no other bandits present. The Tower balcony had been raided. There was an emergency supply cabinet, but it had been pillaged too and there was nothing else worth taking.

A single piece of paper lay on the table. Adonis walked over and picked it up.

"Jesuit," he read.

"Who is that?"

"You know your friend Samson; this is his boss. He is the current leader of the First Constellation. He's heading towards Pavrenes. He's looking for an *imperi,* this note says there is one nearby."

I didn't know what an *imperi* was, but I remembered hearing the name from Olympia on the deck of the *Estonia.* If Jesuit was Samson's boss, he would be even stronger, and the thought made me tremble.

Did we have what it took to beat someone that powerful? Adonis was, of course, stronger than Arabella or me, but I was unsure of how my skill would measure against the leader of the First Constellation.

I did not want to be in a position where I had to rely on someone else's help for victory again, and I did not need to kill Jesuit. I just needed him defeated or scared enough to retreat and that would be enough.

"We need to get there immediately," I said, grabbing Talicia's hand and running down the stairs. Adonis quickly followed.

Looking out at the shore, my eyes fell on Jacob's body. I couldn't just leave him here. It wouldn't be right. He deserved better.

It looked like it was going to rain, and already birds of prey were beginning to congregate above us, eying the corpses below greedily.

"Can you help me put him in the tower? Not at the top, but just past the door. I don't want him getting rained on or left for the crows."

Adonis was silent, before slowly nodding.

With his help, moving Jacob was easier. We lifted him and carefully walked towards the tower. I wished we could have moved all the Pavrenis, but there was no time and Jacob was the one most precious to me.

"I need you to reach out to Arabella again and let her know about the situation. Savant needs to come here as soon as possible," Adonis said, as we walked up the stairs.

"Here is good," I said, pointing towards the cot at the end of the room.

Once we were done, I covered him with a cloth and stepped back, whispering a prayer in his name. Adonis, who'd left me alone with my prayers, was standing at the entrance of the tower.

"Will Arabella and Savant make it in time?" I asked.

Adonis shrugged.

"Even if they don't arrive in time to fight, they can help with rescue and healing.

I nodded, closing my eyes, and extending my mind with magic as I searched for Arabella's mind. Eventually, I found it, but as I tried to make contact, it felt as if Arabella was blocked off. After several minutes, I gave up and opened my eyes.

"No luck?"

I shook my head.

He stepped out of the tower and beckoned me to follow. As we walked through the beach, I scanned for signs of Colden but came up empty.

The night was approaching, so I scanned the shore for boats. Other than a few dilapidated ones that were anchored to the shore, there were few options.

"Do we swim?" I asked, looking up at Adonis, "Talicia won't make it that far and I can't swim well."

"I've got this. Do you see that ship there?"

He pointed and I looked to where his hand was pointing and spotted a boat bobbing in the water.

"The *Aegea*," I said, reading the name on the boat with excitement. "That's one of our boats!"

"Any reason it wouldn't be at the port?"

I shook my head.

"We've never used it that I know of, but obviously a lot has happened these last few days while I've been gone."

"It looks like they're anchored, but we don't know if it's being manned by friend or foe, so we'll need to try to approach unseen. If they are enemies, we seize the boat and sail it directly to Pavrenes, and if they are friendly, we will do the same, just politely. We need to move quickly before they begin sailing again."

"How are we going to get there?" Talicia asked.

Instead of answering Talicia's question, he made his way to the beach's edge. With a deep breath, he manifested his aura and Channeled it toward his hands. With a flick of his wrist, he threw the aura out and it formed a bordeaux-colored bridge just below the water.

Talicia ran forward and stepped gingerly onto it.

"That's so cool," she said, jumping with both feet.

"Don't," Adonis shouted, but it was too late. As she landed on the aura, it shattered, and she fell into the water. I ran into the water and pulled her out.

"It's fragile and thin. It'll support our weight now, but be careful, let's go. Odessa, you lead and keep your sword at the ready."

As I slowly stepped on the bridge, the aura vibrated and hummed but remained intact. Once we were all on it, and the aura remained unbroken, I led us towards the boat.

With Adonis focusing on his aura bridge, I raised my sword and kept my guard up. As the *Aegea* loomed closer, I saw the moving figures within its quarters and on its deck. Whereas the *Estonia* could be managed with two or three people, a boat like the *Aegea* typically required ten or more people to efficiently manage it.

The Aegea was over three times the size of the *Estonia* and had three large sails instead of just one. The sails were rolled up currently and I could see at least four bodies on the deck.

With about a half mile to go, things weren't looking good. Adonis was struggling to hold the bridge. It was beginning to shatter and fade, starting from the Damasyri shoreline.

"How well can you Channel?" I asked Talicia as we traveled. "What did Arabella teach you?"

"Just the basics. I know how to focus on emotions and intent to manifest the aura, but I haven't learned to Channel it properly."

"Okay, I need you to help Adonis," I instructed, holding onto her shoulders firmly. "Channel your aura, focus on transferring, and that should give him some more energy. Go as long as you can, but stop when you get tired, I don't care if it's immediately."

Talicia nodded and she crawled between Adonis's legs and stood up behind him, as gaps appeared in the bridge. Talicia placed her hands on his back and closed her eyes.

Nothing happened at first, but moments later, an orange aura emanated from her and began to cloak Adonis and reinforced the aura bridge.

"Hurry," she cried.

I ran as fast as I could without cracking the bridge further, but Adonis and Talicia could only move so fast while Channeling and remaining touching.

About a quarter mile away, the orange aura vanished, leaving only Adonis's aura. I glanced back worried but saw Talicia still upright and running as fast as she could.

The bridge started cracking under my feet, but the *Aegea* was so close. With one final leap, I grabbed onto the *Aegea's* ladder.

I turned back, just in time to see Adonis lunging behind me. Talicia leaned forward, ready to jump, but at that moment the bridge of aura disappeared, and Talicia was plunged into the dark ocean waters.

"I'll get her," Adonis said, climbing down the ladder and jumping into the water.

As I hung on the ladder waiting, each second felt like an eternity, until finally, Adonis emerged from the water with Talicia wrapped tight in his arm.

He lifted her easily and she grasped the ladder tightly and climbed up to give him space. I hugged her closely.

"I think I saw something down there," she sputtered. She was shivering and I hoped the cold would not affect her too much.

We were so close to my father. We would capture this boat and dock on the eastern shore and get the plagicine to the sick Pavrenis.

I did not want to be whoever was in between me and Grimke. I knew time was short. I needed to be quick, and I would deal with the consequence of any bad decisions after Grimke's safety was guaranteed.

"What did you see?" Adonis gasped, as he slowly made his way up the ladder of the *Aegea.*

"Something big, like a snake," Talicia mumbled.

"Not you," Adonis said, not unkindly. "I mean your sister. How many bandits are there?"

"I haven't looked yet. I was worried about you two," I whispered sheepishly.

He rolled his eyes, pulled out a piece of soggy whey, and began nibbling it.

"Please look now, Odessa."

I climbed up the ladder and peeked my head as low as I could to see who was on the deck. There were now five bandits milling around, laughing and drinking, but what caught my attention most was the person tied to the mast.

His long brown hair had been cut short and faded, and his brown eyes were hidden by his eyelids. His head leaned forward, bobbing up and down, but like his father, I would recognize his face anywhere.

It was Colden.

Chapter ELEVEN

aegea

"They've got Colden."

I felt like my heart was doing somersaults. What was Colden doing here? Was he okay? Did he know what had happened at the Eastern Aid Tower?

Did he know his father was dead?

"Is he alive?" Adonis asked.

I nodded.

"Okay, good. How many hostiles are there?"

I peered up once again, scanning the deck carefully.

"Six above deck."

Looking down at Adonis and Talicia, I studied them carefully. They had both used a significant amount of energy to get us to the ship.

Adonis had eaten some whey so he would be recovered but he had said that it was too much for someone as young as Talicia, so she would remain in her weakened state for a while.

Adonis had handled all previous threats besides Sorbet, but it was two of us against six of them, and any others that lingered in the shadows.

Did we really stand a chance?

"How are you both feeling?"

"We can take them," Adonis said, while Talicia nodded in agreement.

The whey had once again worked its magic and he showed no signs of exhaustion. I saw the confidence and reassurance on his face, and I nodded my head.

"Okay, let's go," I said to Adonis before looking down at my sister. "Talicia, stay here."

"Why?" she complained, but I ignored her.

Adonis and I climbed the ladder. I thought back to the forest, and the fireballs that Adonis had used to take down three bandits at once.

"Adonis," I asked, looking down at him. "How do you hit multiple people with that fire spell?"

Adonis frowned.

164

"The Queen doesn't like dwarves and dwarves don't like hybrids, like us. You should avoid using Dwarven Magic when possible. It uses a different reserve from Channeling, so it's perfect for an emergency, but you should focus on trying to mold your aura better instead. I don't plan on teaching you any further dwarven words of power unless it's an emergency, for your own safety."

With that, he gestured for me to climb onto the deck. Now it was my turn to pout. Colden was being held hostage by a gang of pirates, and if that didn't count as an emergency, I didn't know what did.

We hid behind a ledge, and Adonis gestured for me to go left while he went right. Ithil hung low in the night sky, and the *Aegea* was lit by various torches. I stuck to the dim parts as I made my way toward the first pirate in my path.

I crept behind them and decided to try stealth first. I clamped my hand across the bandit's mouth and then swiped my leg against his legs. He lost his balance and fell. Thinking quickly, I grabbed his head and slammed it against the deck, knocking him unconscious.

One down, five to go.

I continued to hug the shadows as I crept up the deck toward the next bandit in my path. He was a shorter man with a patchy beard. He was leaning lazily against the helm. I couldn't approach him without being seen, as he was leaning quite comfortably against the *Aegea's* wheel.

Remembering how Adonis used his aura to catch me when I fell from the tree in the Montoya Forest, I focused my aura and molded it into a purple hand. Carefully, I extended it across the deck and knocked over a glass bottle.

As the glass shattered, the pirate jumped up, startled. He staggered towards the broken glass. Taking advantage of his distraction, I ran up and swiped his legs from behind. He yelped, and I quickly wrapped my arm around his neck.

He struggled and landed a few blows on my head and leg, but his blows were nothing compared to Samson's. I held on tight until the bandit fainted. Quickly, I dragged his body, but the broken glass had attracted the attention of another bandit who was approaching.

He reached for his sword and opened his mouth to yell, but before the words could leave his mouth, a blade burst through his chest. As he fell, Adonis pulled out his sword from the pirate's back.

"I thought we were in a rush," he said, looking from me to the fallen pirate.

"We are," I whispered, pointing at the other two unconscious pirates. "I was trying to take them out, one by one."

"So was I," Adonis said. He gestured behind him, and I saw the remaining bandits all laying in various crumpled positions on the *Aegea's* deck.

"Show off," I whispered, as he rolled his eyes.

"Check on Colden. I'm going to check below the deck. How many decks are there?"

"Three, I think," I said, thinking back to my sailing days when Grimke taught me about the Aegea. "But I've never been on this boat."

"Okay, well make sure he's okay, then come find me. I may need your help."

As I rushed to Colden, Adonis quietly made his way below deck.

I checked his pulse and breathing. He was alive but unconscious. Using the tip of my sword, I cut the rope and laid him softly on the deck.

"Can I come up yet?" I heard Talicia ask.

I looked up and saw Talicia peeping from Aegea's ladder. I hesitated and looked around at the scene Adonis and I had left behind.

"There's a lot of blood," I said hesitantly.

She shrugged, unaffected.

"My arms are sore," she said, as she climbed onto the deck.

As much as I didn't want her to see the dead bodies scattered on deck, I couldn't leave her on the ladder forever.

"Is he okay?" she said, dropping down beside me.

"I hope so, I think he's just asleep."

167

"What's he doing here?" she asked.

"I'm not-" I started but was interrupted by a loud crash from below deck that vibrated the entire boat.

I looked at the stairs and then back at Colden and Talicia.

"Here," I said, handing her my sword. "Stay with Colden, holler if you need anything. I'll be right back."

"Don't you need it?" she asked, gesturing at my sword.

I shook my head and looked down at my hands.

"I have my magic."

I ran towards the stairs.

"Didn't Adonis say that you shouldn't depend on magic?" she asked.

I ignored her words and focused on my aura as I ran down the stairs. Below deck was dimly lit. There was only one torch hanging and I grabbed it, hoping it would help.

This deck was filled with barrels stacked against the walls. There was one bucket sitting on a chair filled with water and another on the table that smelled of alcohol. The place was quiet. Eerily quiet.

I bumped into something on the floor and cast the torchlight at it. A dead pirate lay on the floor. Other than this, the deck was clear, so I made my way to the other.

The next deck was the crew's sleeping quarters. Two hammocks were hanging on the wall that were dripping with blood. As I made my way closer, I saw the bodies of First Constellation bandits taken in their sleep by Adonis.

I covered my mouth with my hand and continued onwards until I found Adonis crouched in the corner, rummaging through the pockets of one of the fallen pirates.

"Adonis?"

He didn't turn but continued searching through the pockets.

"Is Colden okay?" he asked.

"Yeah, still sleep, but I think he'll be fine with rest," I said, approaching slowly. "I heard a noise down here, so I came to help."

Adonis let the body drop and turned to face me. On his forehead, there was a nasty gash. He dabbed at it with his sleeve, but the moment he cleared the blood, it began to leak again.

"Here, let me try healing that," I offered, but he shook his head.

"Umbari poison," he explained, ripping a piece of the hammock, and wrapping it around his forehead. "It can't be healed with magic. I'll be all right."

The body lying beside him wore a white cape and was dressed in red, similar to Sorbet. I looked up at Adonis, questioningly, but he just gave a tired shrug.

169

"We'll have to save that talk, just like the one about your father. Let's get this boat to Pavrenes."

"Where's your sword?" he asked, as we walked up the stairs.

"I gave it to Talicia."

"If you gave it to Talicia then what were you planning to use?"

I looked away, but he saw the guilt on my face.

He frowned.

"Odessa," he lectured, "You're playing with fire. Don't depend on your magic."

He rummaged through the pockets of one of the bodies on the upper deck and pulled out a dagger.

"Give this to Talicia," he said, passing the dagger to me.

I grabbed the dagger by its hilt and studied it as we walked up the stairs. It was a normal dagger, nothing special, especially compared to the one Talicia had revealed when we first fought the pirates on the *Estonia*.

He paused just before we exited the below decks.

"What is it?" I asked.

"Whispering," he whispered.

"It's probably just Talicia and Colden."

He peeked his head out, before turning back to me with a smile.

"Looks like he's awake."

I ran past him and onto the deck. Talicia and Colden were sitting on the deck, talking. He turned when he heard footsteps and smiled warmly when he spotted me. This was the first time in so long that I ever felt so much joy.

"Odessa," he said, still grinning.

I leaned in and kissed him.

"I was worried about you," I said softly, as I grabbed his face. "I've missed you so much."

"Well, next time I won't leave your side," he replied, pulling me into a hug.

I smiled, relaxing my shoulders, and breathing him in. Being wrapped in his arms was always my safe place.

Once I finally released Colden, Talicia handed me my sword, and I gave her the dagger. Colden tried standing up, but groaned loudly, gripping his side as he fell back onto the floor.

"Let me see," I said.

Colden obliged and pulled up his shirt. He had a nasty puncture wound. I placed my hand on the wound and Channeled my aura. Colden flinched but remained silent as I focused my healing intent. Slowly the wound started closing, until his skin was once again perfectly smooth.

"That's a neat trick." He smiled, rubbing the spot in amazement. "My mother would kill to be able to do something like that. You've got to teach me sometime."

"Yes, but not right now," Adonis interjected, walking towards the helm, "We've got to get this boat moving and it's going to take all of us."

Colden began rising off the ground, but I grabbed his shoulder and held him back.

"Talicia, can you help Adonis?"

Talicia nodded, and with a sigh, she followed Adonis to the helm. She glanced back

I looked into Colden's eyes, rubbing his arms as I struggled to find the words.

"I have some bad news. Do you know about Jacob?"

He looked up, confused.

"My father?" he asked, thinking back. "He took most of the fighters from home and went to the Eastern Aid Tower. You must have seen him on your way here. What did he tell you?"

I hesitated, feeling my stomach drop as I blurted the words out.

"He's dead," I whispered.

Colden dropped my hand, his eyes wide with horror. He shook his head, as his hands began to tremble.

"No, no, no. That can't be. He can't be dead."

He began pacing on the deck.

"I found him on the beach with the other fighters," I explained. "They were all dead except him."

He stopped and turned toward me, in horror.

"So, you let him die," Colden said quietly. It wasn't a question; it was an accusation.

I shook my head and tried reaching out to him, but he stepped back.

"I did everything I could. I tried healing him with my magic."

"Magic?" Colden scoffed. "What about regular medicine? Did you try that?"

Before I could reply, Colden got up and walked away, leaving me alone as he joined Talicia and Adonis near the helm.

"Odessa!" Adonis called. "Get over here."

I got up and walked over to them, avoiding Colden's eyes as he was avoiding mine. If Adonis sensed the tension, he said nothing. Instead, he beckoned me over to the helm of the deck. Talicia looked from me to Colden, curiously, but also said nothing.

"Okay, so a ship like this usually needs more people than what we have here, so we'll need to work together," Adonis instructed and pointed to the various ropes throughout the deck. "We'll need to raise the anchor, angle the sails, and keep the wind as we sail. Colden and I will raise the anchor and get the middle sail, and Talicia and Odessa get the far sail. You'll want to turn until it catches the wind."

Talicia and I walked to the far sail. We both grabbed the rope on each side of the sail to first lower it and then grabbed the second set of ropes to angle the sail until it caught the wind and billowed with life.

Adonis and Colden had raised the anchor and were now working on the massive middle sail.

"Should we help them?" Talicia asked, as the guys shouted instructions to each other.

I looked at Colden and shook my head.

"Let's just give them some space."

Once everything was set and the boat was moving, Adonis grabbed the wheel and guided us to the island. Colden leaned against the side of the boat near the helm and stared at the ocean.

Storm clouds brewed above us. Thunder crackled and lightning flashed in the distance.

The *Aegea* sailed quickly through the water.

Talicia leaned over the side too and let the ocean mist splash her face. I came up behind her and gave her a tight hug as we looked at the island, looming in the distance.

We were almost home.

Chapter TWELVE

ramona

My home was on fire.

We guided the *Aegea* to the island, sailing towards the north shore. The beach was scorched; wrecked boats floated on the shore while the sand was covered with charred wooden stakes and abandoned weapons.

The Queenslen Forest was ablaze. Birds flew out of the fiery trees and animals ran towards the fields. Black smoke spiraled up to the sky.

I ran to the front of the boat, gripping the ledge as I looked at the island in horror. Even though we were still in the water, I could feel the heat of the fire cloaking us as we edged closer. I turned to Adonis, who was steering the ship.

Then we came into the range of the screams. I could hear the cries and shouts from the villagers and bandits in battle even from the sea. My hands trembled, as I stood there, unable to help my people.

He caught my eye and grimaced.

"We're going as fast as we can, Odessa."

Colden strode over and stood beside me, placing his hand over mine. I leaned into him, and he rested his other hand on my back as we both looked at the island.

"With my dad, did you see Tanner?" he asked slowly and quietly.

I shook my head, afraid to make eye contact.

I thought back to the bodies lying on the sand near the Eastern Aid Tower. At the time, I was so focused on Jacob that I hadn't bothered to search thoroughly for other bodies. Everything happened so quickly. But Colden was already angry with me for not saving his father, who knew how he'd respond if I told him this?

"I didn't see him," I admitted, immediately tensing as I waited for the inevitable fallout.

Colden sighed, breaking our embrace, and walking back to Adonis. I wanted nothing more than to tell him the truth; Jacob's wounds were beyond saving, and I still did everything I could to keep him alive. But right now, Colden wasn't ready to hear the truth. He needed space.

As we got closer, Pavrenes became visible on the horizon. Like Opulake, it was ablaze. Bursts of aura lighted the night sky above the village. The battle was still ongoing.

Thunder cracked above us.

I looked up and saw the storm clouds. Lightning flashed, striking the mayor's office. The building burst into flames and screams echoed against the cracks of thunder.

While most of the village was destroyed, the quarantine area where Grimke was resting remained untouched.

I sighed.

At least there's a chance that Grimke's okay.

We were almost at the north shore, so I walked towards Adonis who was still behind the wheel. Colden and Talicia were nowhere in sight.

"Are we going to anchor?"

"No time," he responded, shaking his head as he carefully maneuvered the boat.

"What about an aura bridge?"

He shook his head once again.

"Do you see all that destruction? We'll need all the strength we have. Instead, we're going to whale on the beach. And once we're ashore, I'll search for the bandit captain. I'm certain he's here."

"What about us?" Colden asked as he appeared at the helm with Talicia trailing behind.

"I'd say stay here, but I know this one," he said with a sigh, as he gestured to me. "So I can only say that whatever you decide to do, just be safe. I may not be around to help."

Colden looked at me, his expression grim.

"I have to find Tanner."

I nodded and rubbed my thumb along my sword's hilt.

"I have to find Grimke."

Colden sighed, shifting uncomfortably as he looked from me to the island.

"Odessa," he finally said, "can I talk to you for a moment?"

"A moment is all you may have," interrupted Adonis, as he pointed to the shore that we were rapidly approaching. "Make it quick."

Colden walked to the back of the boat, and I hurried behind him. The moment we were alone, he pulled me into a tight hug.

"I'm sorry about before. I was upset and I lashed out. I know it's not your fault."

He released me, holding my face with his hands as he looked into my eyes.

"I don't want to split up," he whispered. "But I must find Tanner. He might be all I have left."

"Just stay safe, and when you find him, meet me here. We'll be fine."

He leaned in and gave me a soft, warm kiss. I wrapped my hand around his neck and pulled him in. After being held prisoner, forced into battle, and fighting for my life, this moment was everything.

"Grab something," Adonis yelled.

Colden grabbed onto me as the boat crashed and we flew forward. My head would have hit the deck, but Colden had placed one of his hands on my head moments before, so his hand took the brunt of the impact.

Once the boat stopped moving, we got off the floor and ran toward Talicia and Adonis. We spotted them at the helm, with a rope tied to each of their waists and anchored to the mast. Unlike us, particularly Colden's hand, they looked fine.

"Remember what I said," warned Adonis, as he cut the rope off them. "Don't die. We still have much to discuss."

With those words, he ran towards the front of the deck and jumped over the edge without turning back. Talicia grabbed my hand and then Colden's, her tiny fingers trembling.

"I hate splitting up," I said, looking at Colden, "but we have no choice. Can we pray? We need all the help we can get."

Colden shrugged, grabbing my hand, and dropping his head.

"Eloah," I whispered, thinking back to the temple, "please keep my family safe."

"Eloah, eh?" Colden asked, squinting with one eye open. "I think I remember their ministers coming here when we were kids."

When it was over, I released their hands and walked over to my bag, carefully pulling out the box of plagicine.

"Take one of these," I said, passing a vial to Colden. "Just in case."

He examined the vial under the light of a torch. While the other tonic was clear, like water, the plagicine had a golden gleam.

"This is different from the tonics?"

"Better, they're cures. They're called plagicine. If you find your second mother, give her this."

"I wonder if I could replicate it," he continued, as he carefully stowed the vial away.

"It's possible, I mean, your mom probably helped develop it."

I stashed the rest of the vials back in my bag.

"Do you have a sword?"

He shook his head.

Without thinking twice, I lifted my sword and passed it to him. He took the sword reluctantly, pulling it out of the sheath and giving it a quick swish.

"What will you use?"

"I have my magic," I said, emitting some of my purple aura before pointing to my sister, "and Talicia has a dagger."

"Odessa," Talicia retorted, "but Adonis said-"

I flashed her a look and she fell silent. However, this didn't stop her from glaring at me. Since when did she join the Adonis fan club? Even her glare was an uncanny replica of Adonis's.

"Thanks, Odessa, I'll keep it safe."

"Keep yourself safe, first. The sword is a close second."

I pulled Colden into one final kiss, running my fingers through his hair as I tried to memorize every touch. Talicia gagged in the background, but we ignored her.

"Let's go," I said, as we parted.

I grabbed Talicia's hand and walked to the front of the *Aegea*. The boat had crashed at the edge of the beach. The distance from the ledge of the boat to the shore was great; the fall would surely injure us.

181

How did Adonis do it?

"I could probably catch us using my aura or turn it into a stairway."

"How about we just use the ladder?" Colden responded, pointing at the ladder we'd climb on when we first entered the Aegea.

"Right," I said, thankful he couldn't see my flaming cheeks in the darkness.

We made our way to the port side ladder, and I descended first. Talicia followed and Colden after.

The moment my feet touched the sand, I felt at home. After everything, we made it.

It'd only been a few days since we sailed off on the Estonia, but everything was different. The sand was dark with the blood from battle, and the grass and trees nearby were burnt to the ground. It looked eerie and desolate.

"It looks awful," Talicia whispered.

There was nothing I could say to make things better. So instead, I ignored the chills that ran down my body and led her towards our village.

Pavrenes was still a little under a mile from the shore, so we made our way to the hamlet at a brisk jog, and as we reached the eastern edge of the hamlet, the moment of truth arrived, leaving a sinking feeling in my stomach.

The eastern side of Pavrenes was where the quarantine zone was and that was where Grimke was placed, so I was exactly where I needed to be to begin my search. It seemed like most of the fighting was taking place on the western side. But the sounds were drawing closer.

They're pushing this way.

"Where will you head?" I asked Colden.

"If Tanner is here, he'll be with the fighting, so I'll head that way," he said, pointing to the sounds of battle.

"If you see Adonis, try to stick with him," I called, as he ran towards the western side. "He's a good fighter."

He waved his hand before disappearing into the shadows.

"Just us, again," I said, squeezing Talicia's shoulder. "It doesn't look like they've breached the wall yet, but it wasn't built for battle, so we need to be careful and move quickly, okay?"

Talicia nodded, pulling out her dagger and holding it in front of her.

"Let's go save Dad."

We made our way quietly into the quarantine zone. Back when the quarantine zone was being constructed, Grimke had given me a tour of the grounds. There were sections reserved for the sick on one side and a section reserved for the caretakers and medicine on the

183

other. I made my way to the section reserved for the sick. There were two buildings in this section.

"Which building?" Talicia whispered.

"Not sure. Colden and Tanner brought Grimke to the quarantine zone, so we'll just have to check each one."

"Should we split up?" Talicia asked.

"Definitely not," I replied, as we walked towards the building on the right. "Not if we can help it and we don't know if any bandits made it through. I wish I could have left you on the boat, but even that may not have been safe, I'm sure someone heard or saw us crash into the shore when we got here."

As I opened the door, the stench of sickness hit my nostrils instantly. I gagged, holding my breath as I tried to get rid of the smell. Colden's family along with Grimke had been the main ones taking care of the sick. And with his mother in the capital city, his other mother and Grimke lying within these walls, Jacob in battle, Colden captured, and Tanner missing, there was no one left to care for them.

The building was a two-story house with all of the walls knocked down, leaving an open area where many Pavrenis lay on blankets on the floor. The room was filled with wheezing from those struggling to breathe.

"Stay close to me and keep an eye out for Grimke," I whispered.

Pavrenes was small, so I recognized every Pavreni in the room; Asia who always flirted with Grimke, Maia who'd sewn all my clothes my entire life, Graham, the baker, who always added an extra roll of bread in our order. I felt selfish and ashamed, walking past them while carrying the cure to their sickness, but I had to find Grimke first. He was my priority.

We cleared the first floor with no sign of Grimke, and after a quick double check, we proceeded to climb to the second floor.

"You start on the left and I'll check the right."

The sound of a loud crash erupted in the distance, shaking the walls of the building. Screams filled the air, sending a chill through the cold, dark room.

"Quickly," I said, running to the left while Talicia sprinted to the right.

I searched the faces in the room with no luck and met Talicia in the middle. She shook her head as she approached.

"I found Ramona, though," she added.

"Where?"

Talicia turned and led me to her. Ramona's chest rose and fell slowly, her forehead damp.

Colden's lost so much already, I can't stand by and watch him lose a mother.

I got on one knee and slid my bag off my back. Taking a plagicine out of the bag, I carefully uncorked it.

185

Adonis had given me no instructions on the required dosage. The tonic's dosage was the entire vial, and as I tilted Ramona's chin and poured the plagicine into her mouth, I prayed this was the same.

I made sure to get every drop of the plagicine in and then watched silently. She remained unchanged as the seconds passed.

"How long does it take?"

"I'm not sure," I said with a shrug, as I pulled another vial of plagicine out of the bag, "This one is for Grimke. Count to sixty, and if nothing changes, we're going to go to the next building."

"I can do that, but what are you going to do?"

"Well, I want to be efficient with our minute, so while you watch her, I'm going to try to give this cure to as many people as I can."

So, as Talicia began to count, I went to the next body next to Ramona. It was Bentley, a veteran soldier from Jemny. Bentley had always been a grumpy old man, but I knew he was nice at his core, and he told the best stories in all of Pavrenes.

I hesitated with the vial in my hand. On the other hand, Bentley was well into his seventies, even older than Grimke. He had a son named Carson. Although I wasn't the biggest fan of Carson, did he deserve to be without a father? His mother's name was Maya, and she was somewhere here in the quarantine zone too. If I failed to act, Carson could be left an orphan.

Should I save the cure for someone younger? Someone who has their whole life ahead?

I chose to go with my heart instead of my mind.

Once I'd administered the plagicine to Bentley, I moved to the next body. It was Barnabas, the hamlet teacher who had taught me about the other stars besides Astria and Zaniah. He had taught me about things called black holes and supernovas. He knew more about space than anyone else on Pavrenes.

He was also younger than Bentley, and his intelligence would help with rebuilding efforts. I leaned down to give him the cure and gasped.

Oh no, I thought in horror.

Barnabas wasn't breathing. We'd lost a great soul. I covered his face with the blanket and whispered a prayer in his name, before moving on to the next one.

"One minute, and still no change," Talicia called out.

"Okay, this is the last one," I said, looking over at her and pointing to the entrance. "Watch the stairs, and make sure we don't get ambushed."

The third Pavreni was Annalisa, a girl who was a year older than me. I hesitated as I thought of when the girl had pushed me in the Roshni Pond and when I had beaten her in a race when we were kids. I scoffed at the memory. But I couldn't be biased besides Grimke, so I knelt and quickly gave Annalisa the cure.

187

"Okay, let's go," I said, as I met Talicia at the top of the stairs.

She offered me the plagicine I'd given her, but I shook my head.

"Hold on to it, just in case," I said.

Talicia nodded and then quickly slipped the plagicine into her bag.

The power of life and death was too much for me.

Chapter THIRTEEN

pavrenes

We ran out of the right building and made our way quickly to the left. The sounds of battle were louder than before. The sky glowed from the fire and explosions going off in the distance. The shouts and screams of the bandits were getting louder. Their approach was imminent, and I knew we were running out of time.

"Stay close," I told Talicia. She nodded and grabbed onto the hem of my shirt.

We stopped by the door, and I glanced at Talicia one more time before pushing it open and peering inside. This time, I'd brace myself for the scent.

There were more Pavrenis in this room, although there were fewer people in this house than in the first sick house, so the stench was not as bad as before.

As soon as we entered the building, my heart dropped, as I spotted Grimke lying on the floor, in the front of the sick house.

He looked gaunt, his eyes sunken and his cheekbones protruding. His breathing was low and labored. Each breath made his body rattle.

"He's here," I said, and together we rushed towards our father, and I collapsed at his side. Talicia remained standing and peered at Grimke with a worried expression.

I removed the plagicines from my bag and immediately I poured two of the cures into his mouth. I lifted his chin and made sure every drop went down his throat.

Talicia knelt next to me and leaned in for a hug with Grimke, but I caught her arm, freezing her, and shook my head.

"It isn't safe," I said, pulling her back.

She looked at me, questioningly.

"Didn't you give him the cure?"

"We don't know how fast it works or if two will be enough," I explained, with a shrug.

We watched Grimke in anticipation. It felt like time stilled, as his labored breathing continued, with no sign of change. Tears rolled down Talicia's face, and I held on to her tightly as we prayed for our father. After a minute or so, his breathing became less strained, but this was the only change, and he was still unconscious.

I sighed and leaned back, looking up at the ceiling with a small smile.

I did it. I got the cure. Grimke's alive.

Despite all the death and hardship, we had encountered, we were all safe. I wanted to sit there and wait and be there when Grimke awakened, but an explosion in the distance shook the building.

With Grimke safe, my next task was finding Colden. My thoughts flashed back to Eufaula's vision. I needed to hurry.

"Here," I said to Talicia, handing her my bag with the plagicine. "Stay with Grimke and give out these cures to the others until we run out. I think it's a bottle per person. Don't leave this building, no matter what, and if someone comes, you hide and don't fight."

"Wait, where are you going?" Talicia asked, bewildered. "Are you seriously leaving me again?"

"I have to go help Colden and Adonis. They can't do it all by themselves, especially if there's someone stronger than Samson here. They need me."

Talicia's eyes began to water as she wrapped both of her arms around me and pulled me in tightly.

"Please don't leave me alone. I need you. What if Dad dies?"

I took my hand and pulled her chin up until I could see her eyes.

"It's not that I want to leave," I explained, gently. "I'd much rather stay here and make sure he wakes up with you, but I have to go make sure Colden is safe. I need you to be strong, Talicia. I know you've been so strong already, but just a bit longer."

Talicia nodded reluctantly and I squeezed her tightly and glanced at Grimke one last time before I departed.

Once I was out of the building, I realized that the quarantine wall was now breached. The bandits were moving this way and the only thing keeping them from my family and the sick was me.

I manifested my aura as I ran to the quarantine wall. As I got closer, I noticed the man lying on the ground. There was also a huge hole in the quarantine wall.

I cautiously made my way toward him with my aura ready. The closer I got, the more familiar his hair and body looked.

Oh no.

I ran towards Adonis and dropped to my knees beside him. Adonis lay groaning in the dirt, with his hand on his chest. His trousers were untucked from his boots and torn in various places. The black long sleeve shirt he wore under his chest armor was missing its right sleeve and blood leaked through it in several places.

The gate shook and rattled as the bandits shouted and snarled from the other side. Several of them pushed their hands and swords through the Adonis-shaped hole, trying to get through, but luckily it was too narrow.

"Adonis," I said, extending my arm.

"Odessa," he said, as he grabbed my hand.

I pulled him onto his feet. He winced as he rose and clutched the side of his waist where he was bleeding still.

"Need me to heal you?" I asked, leaning closer to inspect the wound.

Adonis shook his head.

"Save your energy, you'll need it for them." He said gesturing to the bandits. "Did you find Grimke?"

I gave him a half smile.

"I didn't think you cared."

Adonis rolled his eyes, but I saw a hint of the smirk he tried to hide.

"I gave him the cure; I think he'll be all right."

"I'm glad to hear that the plagicine works," he said, before stepping closer and shifting my attention to the wall. "Okay, great, I just needed a moment to think. Here's what we're going to do. When the bandits break through, we're going to burst them with a fireball."

"Fussi-" I started, but Adonis cut me off.

"No, that's a fire bolt, less damage, but faster. *Augue* is the word of power you want to use. It creates a fireball, slower, and larger. It is the perfect word for a crowd like this. Wait for my cue. The word will summon the power and you will control it. It's different from Channeling in which you use feelings and emotions. This is Dwarven Magic, so you must wield it, or you will lose control and it will destroy you. That is why you burned your hand before."

I nodded.

It was taking the bandits longer than I thought it would to break through the gate. It seemed they were waiting until the hole was big enough for them all to come through so it wouldn't give us a two-on-one advantage.

Finally, with a loud *crack*, the bandits burst the hole and began to file through the quarantine wall.

My fingers twitched as I began to shape the magic in my body.

"Not yet," Adonis whispered.

There were fifteen bandits and as the last one made it through the gate, the bandits clumped together. They laughed, snarled, and roared with their weapons jabbing and raised in the air.

"Now!" Adonis said and with perfect timing, we both said, "*Augue.*" My hands were seared as a stream of dark purple fire emerged from each of my hands, merged in the middle, and forming an enormous ball of fire.

Adonis's hands were doing the same, although his ball of fire was twice as large as mine and red instead.

The fire hissed and lashed out, reaching for us, and licking our hands and arms.

Adonis angled his fireball into mine and they merged with a massive *hiss*. Despite his fireball being much larger, when the fireballs merged, the new fireball was purple instead of red.

"Push," Adonis groaned, and together we pushed the fireball forward. The giant fireball sped toward dripping flames of fire along the road toward the bandits, who stood frozen in fear.

They cried out and began to fight each other to make it back through the hole in the gate, but it was too late. When the fireball contacted the first bandit, it exploded in a burst of light and flames.

Both my hands were burned with small, uneven circles on my palms. The damage was much less than the first time, but they were still tender. I needed my hands to fight, so even though Adonis had advised against it, I healed my palms using my magic.

Once my hands were healed, I grabbed the piece of wood on the floor and held it out, ready to battle. Colden had my sword, so right now, anything was better than nothing.

A small wave of exhaustion was crashing in my head, clouding my mind, and making me wobble slightly. It was slowly shutting down different sections of my mind and I dropped the wood and struggled to stay standing.

"Good work," Adonis said, as the smoke cleared around us. It appeared that his arms were fine except for a swirling burn that was blistered down his arm.

"Looks like we got them all. Let's go, we need to find Jesuit," he said. "Once we defeat him, the remaining weaklings should flee."

I tried to speak but couldn't. I grunted instead, exhaled deeply, and placed my hands on my knees, trying to calm my speeding heart. The fireball had taken a lot out of me, and I wondered if we would've been better off fighting them one by one. Adonis would be, because he was a great fighter, unlike me.

"You ready?" Adonis asked, and I nodded, even though I was definitely not ready.

I straightened my back and immediately my eyes started to well up with tears. I lost control of my breathing, and my body began shaking. My legs quickly gave in, and I fell to the ground.

"Odessa," Adonis cried, dropping down beside me, "calm down, you're all right. I think you're having an anxiety attack. You've got to calm down and control your breathing."

I tried to reply but my tongue was still on strike. While I tried to calm myself, Adonis got up to fight a pair of bandits that had wandered over. During the battle, he kept glancing over at me with worry.

"Focus!" he said, holding the fingers of one hand up. "Count with me. One, two, three."

With each count, I struggled to time my breaths. By the time I was breathing normally again, Adonis's fight was over. The two bandits were unconscious on the ground.

Tears rolled down my cheeks as I sat up. He extended his arm, which I gripped, and pulled me onto my feet.

"Thanks," I muttered.

I was embarrassed that I'd become so vulnerable in front of him.

"No problem," he said. "I need you. We need to try to minimize your use of magic in the next couple of days. I told you excessive whey use wasn't good. Let's go."

Adonis made his way through the hole in the gate, but as he passed through to the other side, a large hand cloaked in a bright red aura gripped Adonis by the neck and lifted him.

"Fussiladi!" I yelled.

I aimed my attack at the hand holding Adonis. The bolt of fire hit its mark and I heard the yelp of pain from the other side of the wall.

I groaned in pain myself as my right hand was burned raw again. I cursed, gripping the wrist tightly. Muttering, I healed it again.

I felt like I was moving in water, but I picked up the piece of wood and gripped it. I forced myself to run towards the quarantine wall and leaped through the hole in the gate.

On the other side of the gate, Adonis was still being restrained. He struggled weakly against the grip of a bandit man, banging his fist on the man's cloaked arm, but it appeared to not affect him.

His dress was a higher tier than the other bandits and he was as tall as Samson but not nearly as muscular. He had military black hair and dark green eyes.

He tightened his grip on Adonis's neck. I heard a sickening *crack* and Adonis's arms fell limply to his side. His head leaned forward limply. The man lifted Adonis and tossed his body onto the ground in the mud.

I looked at his body in horror.

"Adonis," I cried.

His body remained motionless. Adonis couldn't be dead. He was one of the strongest fighters I knew. He probably could have beat Samson one on one and maybe even Grimke too.

If this man had defeated Adonis, what chance did I have?

I looked around us at the other side of the quarantine wall and saw the hamlet of Pavrenes burning. It was being burned to ashes, and unlike a phoenix, there would be no rebirth for my home.

The buildings were destroyed, and the fighting was over. I was the last fighter.

Odessa and the First Constellation

We had lost.

Chapter FOURTEEN

jesuit

"You're strong," he said, keeping his eyes on me as he pulled out a vial of liquid from his shirt and rubbed it on the spot my fireball had hit. "I can feel it. There's something unique in your blood. Are you really from this nowhere town?"

I ignored him, dropping the piece of wood and staring at the ruined hamlet of Pavrenes. It felt like I was burning along with the buildings.

My memories and dreams were being reduced to ashes. The mission was a failure.

"Ah, well, if you're that upset about this roach of a town, I can put you out of your misery too. I'd hate to; you give off an interesting energy. Killing you would be a shame when we could harness that anger and power. You could be something amazing."

I was the only one left standing. Colden was nowhere in sight, and Adonis was gone. Both were probably dead.

Although we'd only known each other for a few days, I felt I had developed a bond with Adonis. If we were both dwarven, we may have been related in some manner, and he had said there weren't many of us left. But with him gone, I was now lost.

My thoughts turned to Talicia with Grimke. She was waiting for me to come back, but I couldn't see how that could happen and us all escaping.

I would have to delay the man here until they could escape. Hopefully, Grimke would wake up and insist.

I glanced at Adonis, and my heart stopped.

He's breathing! It's weak but he's alive!

As I was lost in my thoughts, suddenly my face was on fire as a force sent me crashing onto the ground. My cheek burned angrily. He had struck my injured cheek with his hand and now it was bleeding again.

"I do not appreciate being ignored," he said with a pleasant looking smile,

He was tall and wore fine leather brown boots and black pants with a red symbol made of scarlet stars. He had a black collar shirt half buttoned up, revealing his chest, and around his neck was a silver and gold necklace with the same symbol on the chain. His shoulders and sides were plated in red metallic armor.

This must have been the bandit captain Adonis had been searching for. Jesuit was his name and I had to assume that he was at least slightly stronger than Samson. Jesuit was their leader and he outranked Samson.

Jesuit must have been smarter and the brains of the operation because he was not as tall or as muscular as Samson had been in the arenas.

His slap had pitched me onto the road, and I had fallen beside Adonis's broken body. Despite Jesuit's damage and claims, Adonis *was* breathing still. There was no doubt about it.

Thinking quickly, I touched my foot against his, focusing my aura to heal him. I needed to distract Jesuit long enough for this to work.

"Who are you? What do you want from me? From us?"

"That's better, nothing wrong with a bit of conversation." He smirked. "I am Jesuit, leader of the First Constellation. What I want from you is to see if you're strong enough to be one of us. And what I want from this pitiful town is nothing. It's just business."

Business? They destroy lives for business?

My magic was beginning to dwindle, but I emptied most of what I had left into Adonis. It appeared to have worked after Adonis coughed slightly.

Jesuit narrowed his eyes at his body. I stood up slowly, trying to keep his attention. I needed to stall as long as I could until Adonis could get up and help fight. He seemed interested in me; I would play into that.

"Why would I ever join murderers like you?"

"Who said it was optional?" He laughed, gesturing at the inferno around us. "You either join or die."

Jesuit raised his glowing red arm, opened his hand, and aimed his palm at me.

"Which shall it be?"

I'd used most of my aura healing Adonis, and Colden had my sword, but I needed to protect Talicia and Grimke, and the only thing left was the piece of wood on the ground. I grabbed it and held it up in defense.

Jesuit charged towards me, his hand raised and his red aura glowing. I stood my ground, waiting. Once he was near, I ducked and swung the wood toward his legs. He jumped, avoiding it, and pulled the wood out of my hand. Splinters of wood dug into my hands.

I blocked my face with my hands, just as he swung the wood at my head. A thin layer of purple aura appeared but was quickly cracked and the wood slammed into my head.

I fell to my knees, clutching my head.

"Maybe I was wrong about you," he said with a smile, as he discarded the piece of wood.

I stood unsteadily and looked up. Just over Jesuit's shoulder in the distance, a hazy figure appeared. I squinted to make sure I was hallucinating and saw that the hazy figure was Tanner.

He was alive. I looked at his surroundings, but Colden was nowhere to be seen. Had Eufaula's vision already happened?

Jesuit aimed a punch at my shoulder, but I ducked and punched him in the chest. We continued sparring, and it soon became clear that this was all a game to him. He was playing with me.

I aimed another kick at him, but he jumped and landed on my leg.

Crack.

I screamed as the pain erupted from my leg. Using my hands, I dragged myself away from him and Channeled my magic to my broken leg. My aura appeared but quickly fizzled out. My reserves were low, and I knew that extending them would kill me.

"A healer, that's impressive."

I winced through the pain, searching for Tanner, but he'd disappeared. And with Adonis unconscious, I was alone.

"What will you try next?" Jesuit taunted. "Will your body give up first or your spirit? I wonder."

He raised his foot again and brought it down, aiming at my chest. I rolled away, dragging myself towards Adonis, and Jesuit let out an evil cackle.

"Come on, Adonis, wake up," I muttered, shaking him.

"That Mystio is done for," Jesuit sneered as he walked towards us. "I felt his neck crack in my hand. He was a skilled fighter and would've been a powerful addition, but the Mystio are stupidly loyal to their own. It's either they join or die. Those are your options."

"We'd rather die!"

Colden and Tanner were running toward us with Talicia not far behind them. It was Colden that had said the words. He swung his sword at Jesuit while Tanner managed to dive between his legs.

Jesuit leaned back and avoided Colden's slash easily, but Tanner struck him hard in the head with a long piece of metal.

Jesuit looked surprised and then his eyes rolled back into his head, and he fell to the ground.

Talicia rushed over to me and placed her hands on my leg. An orange aura erupted from her hand and made its way toward my wound. Once the wound was healed, we both joined Tanner and Colden who were standing over an unconscious Jesuit.

"Take this, Odessa," Colden said, passing my sword to me.

Talicia bent over Adonis and Channeled into him. She sent her orange aura into his chest, and after a moment he stood up.

"That's all I can do," she muttered, and I told her it was okay. My leg was sore, but her healing had helped me. I wondered when Adonis had told her how to heal because I hadn't done so.

Colden and Tanner grabbed Adonis and lifted him onto their shoulders. The four of us made our way through the hole in the quarantine wall and halted in front of the building with Grimke in it.

"Where are we going?" Tanner asked.

"We sailed the *Aegea* here," I said, leading the way towards Grimke. "We didn't park very well, so hopefully it's still sailable, but we need to get the four of us plus Grimke and anyone else we can fit onto the boat. We must be quick and do it before more bandits get here. They may have boats, so we'll need to keep an eye out for that too."

"Good plan, Deputy Mayor," Colden said with a smile. "Come on," he said to Tanner. "I know where we 'docked'."

Colden and Tanner rushed off with Adonis on their shoulders to where we'd crashed the *Aegea,* leaving Talicia and me behind.

"Okay, you're going to help me move Grimke and then stay on the *Aegea*. I mean it this time. Jesuit or other bandits could show up at any time and we can't beat them."

Talicia pouted but nodded her head as we entered the second sick house. We went directly to Grimke and attempted to lift him, but because of our height difference, it was difficult to put him on our shoulders as Colden and Tanner had done previously.

"Grab his feet, and I'll grab him by the shoulders," I instructed.

Once we had him, we both made our way out of the building.

"How many people did you get the cure to?" I asked her.

"I wasn't keeping count," Talicia admitted. "I got everyone in this building and there were still plagicines leftover. I was going outside to the other building to do more but then I heard you scream, so I came to help, but I bumped into Colden and Tanner first. They told me to wait."

"The whole building, that's good. Excellent job, Talicia."

We reached the door archway and crossed the threshold. Suddenly, a large hand hit me and sent me flying backward. Jesuit emerged, standing over me. Blood poured from his nose and a cut on his cheek. He growled and swung a long-curved blade at me.

"You have chosen death!" he roared. "I'll kill everyone on this unnamed island!"

I blocked his attack with my sword. He was so strong and swift that the only thing I could do was stick to defense.

Talicia yelled my name.

"Stay back!" I screamed, frantically.

She jumped over Grimke's body and aimed her orange aura at Jesuit.

"Fussiladi!" Talicia shouted.

No fire emerged, but her aura did burst forth and push Jesuit's chest. Yet, he remained unmoved. He howled with laughter, forgetting me, and focusing on Talicia.

"Dwarven Magic! Where did you learn such words of power, little one? Maybe I should take you instead."

I forced myself to stand and gripped my sword with both hands. My hands were still sore, but I manifested my aura once more. It flared to life but flickered faintly.

"Leave her alone," I said.

"Odessa!" Talicia cried.

"You are clearly out of power; this feeble display of magic isn't fooling anyone," he said. He shook his head pitifully at me. "I could show you what true power is!"

He raised his fist and his red aura flared to life as his eyes sparked with electricity. He raised an open palm, and out of a storm cloud above us, a bolt of golden lightning emerged and struck his palm.

His palm buzzed with energy, and it felt like the air itself was burning. Jesuit pushed his hand forward and sent the bolt of lightning toward me.

I panicked and lifted my sword in an attempt to stop the attack.

I looked in awe as my sword absorbed the energy and the black metal turned to gold. The energy radiated from the sword and trickled into me. I could feel myself recharging, but unlike the whey, which left me fully energized, this felt like a temporary boost.

The lightning spiraled around the blade, going up my arms, and soon my entire body was surrounded by lightning. Jesuit took a step back, in horror, but Talicia activated her aura just for a second and pushed him toward me. I gripped my sword tightly and aimed the blade at Jesuit.

Jesuit stumbled back, speechless. That ugly grin left his face as the tip of the blade connected with his chest armor; the energy erupted from the sword and arced across Jesuit's body.

Pieces of metal leaped from his chest in small bursts of lightning and Jesuit howled in pain, trying to remove the armor, with little success. He balled his fist and closed his eyes, trying to absorb the lightning as his face contorted in pain.

When the blade was empty of lightning, I dropped it. I didn't want to give him any time to recover, so I circled Jesuit, moving away from Talicia and out in the open. This was my battle, and no one else was going to get hurt.

As the lightning began to fade, he turned to face me and lifted his palm again. Thunder roared, but before he could summon another bolt of lightning, I placed my palms together on his chest.

"Augue!"

A ball of dark purple fire sprung from my palms and blasted into Jesuit. It sent him flying toward the ocean. Colden, Adonis, and Tanner ducked underneath the ball of fire as it roared over them.

The fireball stopped burning over the ocean, and I watched as Jesuit's body fell into the water. I bent down to retrieve my sword; Jesuit's chain was attached to it. I unraveled it and pocketed the chain.

Colden and Tanner ran over while Adonis trailed slowly behind. Colden pulled me into a hug while Tanner checked on Talicia. Adonis didn't speak, but just nodded at me and gave me a thumbs up.

He then nudged his head to my right, and I followed his gaze to Grimke, who was still lying on the floor. I released Colden and ran toward him with Talicia and the rest following closely behind.

Grimke was stirring. His eyeballs moved behind his closed lids and his fingers twitched.

I dropped to my knees and gently touched his face.

"Grimke?"

His eyes fluttered open.

Chapter FIFTEEN

colden

Grimke's blue eyes shifted from Talicia to me. He lifted his hands slightly and tried sitting up, but he was still weak. I grabbed his shoulder, helped him up, and pulled him into a hug.

"Grimke!"

He patted me on the back gently, before opening his arm and pulling in Talicia. She whimpered and squeezed us both. I couldn't stop the tears that flowed down my cheeks.

Despite the loss of the hamlet itself, my father had prevailed. He had gotten the cure. We did it. My father was alive. We had saved him.

I looked up at Tanner and Colden who were standing above us. Tanner smiled and Colden placed his hand on my shoulder affectionately.

"Ramona's in there," I said, pointing to the first quarantine building. "I gave her the plagicine already too."

Tanner nodded and ran into the first quarantine building with Colden following closely. He limped after his brother, and I watched him with concern.

Once we released Grimke from our embrace, Talicia stood and stepped back. I followed suit and Adonis helped me pull Grimke to his feet. Once we were each supporting him on opposite sides, we slowly made our way to the *Aegea*.

The power I'd gained from the lightning was now gone, and as we walked through the sandy shore, waves of exhaustion were washing over me.

"How are you feeling?" I asked Grimke.

"Lucky to be alive," he replied with a hoarse laugh. "Thank you, Odessa. You've become such a strong woman. I'm so proud of you."

I mumbled an incoherent thanks, aware that my cheeks were now red. My father gave praise rarely, so when he said it, I knew he really meant it.

I did not have as high an opinion of the results of my quest. Yes, my father was safe, but so many Pavrenis were dead, and we were fleeing our home.

Pavrenes would be left in the hands of the First Constellation. They would stay here and continue to destroy and pillage, but even if they left the island, nature would pick up where they had left off, and soon the buildings would sink into the ground and the streets would become overgrown and abandoned.

"Are you okay?"

I looked at Adonis, who'd been silent the entire time.

"I thought you were dead," I continued.

He pointed at his throat before covering his mouth with his hand.

"You can't talk?"

He nodded, as his face turned somber.

"Do you want me to heal it?"

Adonis shook his head quickly. He manifested a weak aura and shook his head again.

"No more magic, got it."

Although I felt sorry for his predicament, I was secretly relieved that he'd said no to my help. My body felt so drained, and I was using every ounce of energy I had left to make it back to the boat. I needed time to rest, which meant that he'd be without a voice until we reached Fort Mudo and someone else could heal him.

"Odessa!"

Colden and Tanner stopped beside us. Tanner was holding his mother, Ramona, who was still unconscious.

I walked closer to the quarantine gate and beckoned Colden to follow.

"Once Ramona is safely on the *Aegea*, I want you and Tanner to bring the others from the sick house back to the boat. Adonis, Talicia, and I need to speak to Grimke, alone."

"Everything okay?" Colden asked, worried.

I nodded, though I was sure my face said otherwise, because Colden's frown deepened, and he grabbed my hand.

"I have questions about my magic that only Grimke can answer."

Adonis looked up at us at that moment. He either had sensitive hearing or had guessed our conversation because when our eyes met, he nodded.

Colden followed my gaze and his hand stiffened.

"Adonis has to be there," I explained. "He also has questions. I'll explain everything once we're sailing."

With those words, Colden relaxed, and we both walked back to the group. Then, Colden and Tanner made their way to the *Aegea*, with Ramona.

When it was just the four of us, I turned to Grimke, who was scuffing Talicia's hair.

"We need to talk."

Grimke sighed and nodded. I sat on the ground and Talicia dropped down beside me, while Adonis remained standing.

"I need to know where my mother is," I asserted. "And I need the truth."

Grimke fell silent. Talicia looked from him to me, confused. But we all remained silent as we waited.

"You may not remember this," he finally said, "but your mother left several times throughout your childhood. Sometimes she told me ahead of time, sometimes she did not, but she always came back. When she left this last time, she didn't tell me. She grew up in Cypress, but I don't think that's where she went."

"My mother was a Cypressian? Why wasn't I told this?"

"Because you'd want to leave, and you weren't ready."

"And now I am?"

He gestured to me and my sword.

"Look at how much you've grown, Odessa. You saved us."

Grimke smiled, his pride reflected in Talicia and even Adonis's expressions.

"I trained you as best as I could, and you've utilized this and your own skill to become the fighter you are. You're ready to find your mother."

Colden and Tanner returned from the *Aegea*, but they passed by and continued toward the sick house.

"Okay, Gr- Father," I continued. "Is my sword really called Backstabber? Are you really a dwarf? Did you really kill the dwarf king?"

"I am a dwarf, and I did kill the tyrant king, Potiphar. And because of this, others have renamed this sword Backstabber."

"Why did you kill the King?"

It seemed my concept of who my father was had been completely fabricated, and he had forged a mirage of a new identity that hid his misdeeds.

"The war against the humans was going badly. They had already destroyed Alabanza and Hominy. The human ruler High King Nairobi and Potiphar had taken the High King's family hostage. He had already encased Nairobi's mother in *sebi*, which is a liquid rock that hardens around the victim. He did this to many who displeased him and kept them all in a large hall. The other clans were allied under Potiphar, and despite Nairobi's deal to allow the dwarves to live in Damasyr in peace, Potiphar refused and began the execution of the High King's family. I was too late to save his mother, but I slayed the High King and the clans fell into disarray without his leadership. The High King retrieved his family and honored the previous agreement and allowed the dwarves to leave and even kept some in his court. Some clans continued to fight until the end, but some dwarves escaped to the east and south, some to their hidden underground cities. It was not until Nairobi's son,

Psalm, was overthrown by the current dynasty that dwarves began to be hunted."

Grimke finished speaking and I was silent. He had said a lot and I thought about it. He had murdered someone not in self-defense but for the supposed greater good.

Tanner and Colden were coming out of the sick house with another Pavreni, and I recognized Carson on their shoulders.

"Are you okay?" Colden called and I nodded.

I watched as he and Tanner hurried to the *Aegea.* Adonis was already helping Grimke to his feet, so I ran over and took hold of his other shoulder.

Together, we made our way to the *Aegea* with Grimke on our shoulders. We passed Colden and Tanner running back to the village and I smiled at them.

Once we were in front of the *Aegea*, I passed Grimke to Talicia.

"Help Adonis," I instructed. "I'll go back to the village and help Colden and Tanner. Talicia, you'll stay with Grimke."

I ran back to the village, but as I got closer, I noticed Tanner and Colden running toward me. Tanner was carrying a girl named Victorija in his arms while Colden was waving a sword. Behind them, was a group of bandits chasing after them with raised weapons.

I jogged towards them, just as one of them threw a spear. It zoomed through the air towards Colden and pierced his thigh.

"No," I screamed as he fell to the ground with a wail.

Tanner stopped but Colden waved him off. Reluctantly, Tanner continued as Colden struggled to remove the spear.

Tanner ran past me towards the *Aegea* trusting his brother's fate with me. I got close to Colden and glanced at the members of the First Constellation.

"Odessa," Colden pleaded, as I drew nearer and ran past him towards the bandits. "Leave me and save yourself."

The bandits faltered for a second, confused. It was twelve full-grown men against a teenage girl. To them, this was probably an easy win.

"Jesuit is gone. I defeated him. And I'll defeat you. Leave now and I'll let you live," I said, as I stopped before them and held out my sword. Within seconds my sword turned purple as I Channeled my energy.

The bandits looked to the back of their group and moved aside as a woman stepped forward.

"It's you." I gasped.

It was the woman from the *Estonia*. While the other bandits looked dirty and injured from battle, her clothes were still pristine and her face untouched.

"My, my, look how you've grown," Olympia said with a smirk.

She towered over the other bandits, and by the way they all looked at her and waited; she was their leader. She stepped closer, sweeping her dark hair over her shoulder.

"I will say your bluffs haven't gotten any better," she said with a shrug.

"I'm not bluffing."

"Do you really expect me to believe that you met and defeated Jesuit?"

I lifted Jesuit's necklace in the air. Ithil's light illuminated the First Constellation pendant and reflected the constellation onto the ground.

"Don't do anything silly now," I said with a smile.

Olympia frowned, looking from the necklace to me, before turning swiftly and walking back towards Pavrenes.

"Let's go," she said. "Do one more search and then meet at the *Sea Queen.*"

"But Lieutenant Captain-" one of the bandits started. Before he could finish, she plunged a dagger into his gut.

"It's just Captain now," she said.

She walked away back towards the destroyed hamlet without another word or backward glance with the other bandits quickly following her.

I held my stance until they all disappeared and dragged myself to Colden and dropped myself beside him on the sand.

"Are you okay?"

I couldn't help but laugh as I looked at him and saw the worry on his face.

"You're the one with the spear protruding from your leg," I said, pointing at the spear.

He rolled his eyes but said no more as I tried to Channel my aura to heal his wound. A faint hint of purple erupted from my fingertips before quickly disappearing.

"Okay, plan B," I said, as I tore the bottom of my shirt off. "This is going to hurt."

I wasn't sure it was a promising idea to remove it but there was no way I could transport him with a spear that was taller than me in his leg. Colden winced as I gripped the spear, but he nodded his head.

I considered a countdown but thought better of it and just pulled the spear out of Colden's leg and immediately tied the piece of my shirt just above his wound high and tight as a makeshift tourniquet.

Colden grunted in pain, as he stood up and gingerly tested his weight on his wounded leg.

"Can you pass me the spear?"

I picked it off the sand and gave it to Colden, who used it as a walking stick and took a few tentative steps forward. His pace was slow, but it was the best we could do in our current predicament.

We limped together along the road, and I began to think about how many people we could fit on the *Aegea*. Could the boat even sail? And even if it could, where would we go?

"Are you okay?"

I was silent for a moment as I thought over his words. *Was I okay?*

"Yes," I finally answered. "It's just a rough patch. But we'll get past it. I'm just glad you and my family are alive and safe."

His face darkened at my words, and he looked at the ground.

"I told Tanner about our father; we're going to go get his body and bury him here."

I nodded. With bandits still roaming the streets, Pavrenes wasn't safe, but I knew Jacob would want to be buried here and it was not like I could stop the brothers.

I thought of Jacob's wives Ramona and Reyna and wondered once again if Reyna was safe in Jemny or on her way home. She would be expecting her home and family to be in one piece. Instead, she would find Pavrenes burned and ruined and with all the Pavrenis dead or gone.

I squeezed Colden's arm affectionately and he smiled at me. He struggled to kiss me on the cheek, but it still left a warm feeling inside me.

"Come on, we've got to get out of here," I said with a smile. "There will be plenty of time for kissing later on."

"Promise?" He grinned.

"Look, there's Adonis and Tanner," I said gesturing to the two figures rushing up the road. "I'm just glad Talicia stayed on the ship."

I glanced back behind us periodically to make sure the bandits didn't come back as we moved until we met up with Adonis and Tanner.

"What did you do?" Tanner asked, relieved to see we were both okay.

"I bluffed," I replied, with a half-smile.

"So, what's the plan now?"

"Does the boat float?"

Adonis nodded, as Tanner said, "It's good to get us to the mainland. Although I'd like to know who anchored it in the first place."

I chuckled as he side-eyed Adonis who suddenly interested in the clouds above us.

"Well, Talicia gave the plagicine to everyone in the second sick house, so we should load as many of them onto the *Aegea* as we can and sail for the mainland. And before we leave, we should give the rest of the

222

plagicine to as many people as we can, but I don't think we'll have room. They'll have to take the *Salia*. Hopefully, it's still there."

"What about the sick?" Colden asked.

"We shouldn't mix the sick with those who've gotten the plagicine," I replied, shaking my head at him, "Come on, you know that. We'll have to leave them here too."

Colden nodded, though clearly displeased with my answer. But with our limited supply of plagicine, there was little else we could do.

"Maybe one of us should stay here with them," he suggested.

I frowned, but before I could speak, Tanner said, "I don't see the point of that, Colden. If nothing can cure them but the plagicine, we should try to get more plagicine and bring it back here for them as soon as we can. If any cured Pavrenis don't fit, we can bring them back when we come back to bury Dad."

"Okay, that's the plan; let's get to it," I said before Colden could further argue his point.

Adonis and Tanner walked past us towards the sick house, and I escorted Colden to the *Aegea*.

The *Aegea's* hull was severely damaged, but it had fallen back into the water and was bobbing up and down with the waves. As we neared the boat, I realized that we'd need to climb the ladder to get aboard, something that'd be impossible for Colden.

223

"Odessa!"

Talicia was smiling down at me, standing next to Grimke as they both waved down at us. Grimke managed to climb down the ladder and help Colden onto the deck.

"Colden, please stay here with Talicia, and before you protest, you know you shouldn't be walking on that leg."

To be fair, with all the energy I exhausted, I knew I shouldn't be walking either, but Tanner and Adonis needed help.

"Grimke if you're able to, we're going to be bringing some Pavrenis with us, and we could use your help," I said.

"Look, we made these," Talicia said, running over and gesturing to a large piece of fabric attached to two long pieces of wood. They were makeshift stretchers. There were three in total, and they would make the long walk from the boat to the sick house more efficient.

"They'll work great," I said, patting Talicia on her shoulder as she gleamed with pride.

It was impossible to carry the gurney and my sword at the same time, so I leaned my sword against the edge of the boat by the ladder. Grimke and I slowly brought the stretchers down the ladder of the *Aegea* just as Adonis and Tanner arrived with some Pavrenis.

I showed them the stretchers Talicia and Grimke had made and together the four of us went back to the sick houses to bring as many people as we could onto the boat.

The First Constellation all seemed to have left the island and by sunrise, we had gotten everyone out of the first sick house and onto the Aegea and had also distributed the remaining twelve plagicines to the other sick Pavrenis.

While the others prepared the boat, I ran over to our village and left two notes: one in front of our own house and the other in front of the derelict remainder of Colden's home. The letter left a summary of what had happened and made it known that we were heading to the mainland.

As I stood in front of my house and stared sadly at our broken village, I thought back to last week when I stood here and addressed the village. So much had happened since then, so much destruction and so many lives lost.

Colden appeared next to me and wrapped his arm around me.

"Why does no one listen to me?" I said, feigning frustration, as I leaned into his hug. "Come on, aren't you the doctor's apprentice? You *know* you shouldn't be walking on that leg."

"I had to say goodbye too," he said somberly. "I always thought that this is where my heart was, and I couldn't live anywhere else. But now I look at this and know. I know my heart is wherever you are. You are my home."

225

We stood in silence, holding each other as we said goodbye to our old home.

The wind shifted suddenly, and the door to the stables swung open and banged against its frame. The only building left unmaimed was the stable house. I thought of Scout and went over to see if he was there, but he and all the other horses were gone.

I hope you're safe wherever you are.

After quickly looting the town for what little the bandits had left behind, Colden and I returned to the *Aegea.* Together, we loaded all of the supplies onto the Aegea and set sail.

All the sick Pavrenis were housed below deck and the five of us milled around on the top deck. Grimke took control of the helm and began to sail us around the island and west towards the mainland. Adonis managed the sails and made sure the angles were right so that they always caught the wind. Talicia had climbed the crow's nest to enjoy the view and I lay on the deck next to Colden.

Colden had fallen asleep after we had all joined on the boat and I watched him with worry. His leg wound needed medical assistance but collectively we knew little of medicine or what we should do next besides covering the wound, and no one had the magic to heal him either.

As I looked up at the sky, I searched for the constellation on Jesuit's necklace, but couldn't find it.

My eyes grew heavy. It had been days since I'd gotten a restful sleep, and with everyone else taking charge, I closed my eyes and drifted off.

I fell asleep thinking about space and the names of other stars and planets.

o

I awoke to the sound of thunder.

I saw we had not traveled far from the island and figured I couldn't have been sleeping for long. I tried to recall my dream but all I remembered was a white moon hanging in a black sky.

I sat up frantically and looked around. The sky was black like my dream, but Ithil was hidden by tremendous dark clouds.

I felt my heart sinking into my stomach. I glanced at Colden and saw he had dozed off on my shoulder. He was awake and was frozen next to me with a look of horror on his face.

"What's going on?" I asked him, but he didn't answer.

It appeared he tried to speak but no words came out. He instead pointed and I followed his finger and gaze and saw at the top of the ladder was Jesuit.

His skin was scorched and burned, and his clothes had lost their elegance and hung loosely on him in strips and tatters. Seaweed hung off his shoulder and all that remained of his left hand was a burned stump.

I watched in horror as he raised what remained of his arm into the sky and a bolt of lightning streaked toward him. I looked frantically for my sword and saw it leaning against the side of the boat, next to Jesuit.

Oh no.

I tried to move but my body refused to obey. My adrenaline had worn off and my legs ached.

Jesuit grinned and aimed his palm at me. I saw the golden lightning streak toward me. Out of the corner of my eyes, I saw Grimke and Adonis running toward me.

Time was moving so slowly; I could see the different arcs of the lightning as they traveled toward me. It was terrible, but it soon became worse when Colden rolled on top of me.

"What are you d-"

I tried to push him off of me, but I was exhausted.

"Happy birthday," Colden said, and with great difficulty, he quickly pulled out the silver and amethyst bracelet I had seen at Merica's shop during the merchant festival. "I love you."

He pushed hard against the deck, throwing his body up, and took a half step over, intercepting the bolt of lightning. His body spasmed from the energy as the lightning arced across his body and made his hair stand.

Jesuit howled with laughter, as I looked on in horror.

Colden strained to turn his head back and looked me in the eyes. I could tell he was in pain, but he smiled at me anyways, and when his body hit the ground and stopped moving, he was still smiling.

Chapter SIXTEEN

talicia

I screamed.

It should've been me.

I had to save him.

I could heal him.

If only my body would move.

Move!

Adonis and Grimke approached Jesuit with their weapons drawn. Everything was moving in slow motion, and I felt as if I was back under Eufaula's thrall in the Montoya Forest.

I watched as Tanner knelt over Colden's body and the tears rolled down his face, confirming what I already knew. Jesuit climbed up the ladder and stood on the deck. As he approached, Adonis took a half step back, but Tanner stood up and charged Jesuit.

While Colden was the skinnier brother, Tanner worked more with his father and was bulkier. His muscles flexed as he grasped onto Jesuit and attempted to grapple him and throw him overboard.

Tanner's maneuver didn't faze Jesuit, and without a word, Jesuit slapped Tanner hard on the back of his neck with his good hand and Tanner fell to the deck with a thud. Tanner's eyes fluttered quickly for a moment, and then they closed.

Grimke sidestepped Tanner's body and stabbed forward with a sword he'd found onboard. It was nothing like my black bladed sword, but Grimke was proficient with most weapons.

Grimke managed to sink his sword into Jesuit's chest, but Jesuit only laughed manically and raised his hand in the air. Grimke ducked, anticipating a blow to the head, but Jesuit instead aimed for Grimke's arm.

Jesuit's fist slammed onto Grimke's wrist with a sick *crack,* his sword clattered onto the deck of the *Aegea.* Grimke stumbled back and I watched in horror as Jesuit wrapped his arms around Grimke and began to squeeze. Jesuit, keeping his grapple, turned his good hand upwards, and I knew what was going to happen next.

Adonis moved forward quickly and slashed at both of Jesuit's arms with his sword, but Jesuit still held on tightly to Grimke.

231

Thunder roars filled the sky, as the storm clouds swirled, and the air burned. Another bolt of lightning shot down from the sky, leaping around Jesuit and Grimke who was still wrapped in his arms in frantic spirals.

Grimke's head shot back, and he groaned in pain. He managed to pull the sword across Jesuit's chest, which caused the gash to deepen, but Jesuit squeezed him even tighter, and the blade clattered onto the deck.

I heard footsteps running towards us. Talicia stopped beside me and gasped. Grimke was restrained. Tanner was unconscious. Adonis was watching Jesuit closely, waiting for a moment to strike. And Colden was-

Talicia, no, I tried to say, but my mouth still refused to move. I was sweating profusely and knew I was near my limits. I needed power, more power. I closed my eyes and extended my mind.

Arabella.

I didn't feel anything at first. She might have been too far for our empathy link, or I was out of magic, or both. I was just going to give up when I felt Talicia's hands on my shoulders.

"Here, take my magic! Quick, Dad's gonna die," she said, through tears.

I felt her magic flowing into me and I absorbed it all. It wasn't much but it allowed me to move, and I only needed a spark. I knelt and reached out again.

Arabella!

Odessa!

I felt Arabella's cool presence in my mind. Her mind was not as tranquil as usual, I could feel her pain. She was hurting.

Are you okay? I can feel the pain you are in. Do you need help?

Arabella, I need your power, it's an emergency. I need more magic. Please.

I felt Arabella hesitate and then felt her power flow into me.

Here. Be careful, Odessa.

Thank you, I said quickly.

Of course.

I quickly crossed the deck and grabbed my sword. Jesuit saw that I was standing and stopped his laughing.

He continued to shock Grimke, who was now silent with his head leaning forward. Jesuit aimed his hand at me, and I raised my sword, ready to counter the lightning again.

He stopped, remembering what happened last time.

Instead, he aimed past me and fired a smaller bolt of lightning. I jumped to the left and extended my arm and the sword as far as it could go, attempting to catch the bolt, but it was faster than me and I was still sluggish. I missed the bolt of lightning and fell onto the deck in horror as the energy flew past me toward Talicia.

"No!" I yelled, but I knew it was too late.

Talicia raised her hands to cover her face and screamed, but just before the bolt hit her, Adonis appeared at her side, shouldering her out of the way and taking her place instead.

His mouth opened and closed in pain, but no sound came out, and after a few seconds, he fell to the ground, spasming with a few remaining sparks of lightning traveling throughout his body.

Talicia knelt at his side and touched Adonis's arm. She yelped as she was shocked by the static that remained on his body.

I tightened the grip on my sword and charged toward Jesuit. He saw me coming and released his grip on Grimke who fell to the ground too. Jesuit quickly raised his hand, but the bolt took longer than it usually did.

I took advantage of the buffer and swung as hard as I could. Jesuit's lower arm fell onto the deck with a wet thud. I knew he could still conjure lightning without his hands, so as he doubled over in pain, I didn't hesitate to raise my sword and aim it at his neck, bringing it down as hard as I could.

My sword bounced back as it contacted Jesuit's cherry red aura. The edge of my sword glowed red with tinges of Jesuit's aura, and before he could raise his head, I growled, lifted my sword, and swung again, digging into Jesuit's aura.

The aura was absorbed by my sword, and it began to glow more vibrantly, as if it was feeding on the magic. My third swing got in even deeper, reaching just above Jesuit's skin, but he didn't let me get a fourth try.

Jesuit stood up tall, towering over me, with his aura covering his entire body. He quickly raised his cloaked leg and kicked me hard in the side. The blow sent me flying and I crashed into the side of the deck.

I'd lost my grip on my sword and I searched for it frantically, worried Jesuit might use more lightning. Jesuit kicked me hard in the stomach and sent me rolling until I landed at Talicia's feet.

I looked up and saw that she was holding Grimke's bandit sword in her right hand and had her left hand balled.

"No," I murmured, but Talicia stepped over me and approached Jesuit. The sword she held was much too long for her, and she leaned it on her shoulder to support the weight.

"I'll kill you and everyone on this boat," he warned. "I know I look rough, but you are sorely mistaken if you think you can beat me, little one."

Talicia didn't answer, and instead, she swung the sword with a grunt. The sword traveled toward Jesuit slowly and he made an exaggerated dodge and said, "Oops, so close."

It was no later than the words left his mouth that Talicia swung her balled hand and released a hand of something granular right in Jesuit's face, just as she must have witnessed me doing to Samson during my fight with him.

Jesuit roared as the grains landed in his eyes.

Talicia struggled to lift the sword and I got up and dashed over. Together, we aimed the sword and sank the blade into Jesuit's stomach, slashing horizontally.

I didn't want to kill him, but I couldn't risk him coming back again. Jesuit went quiet; he didn't speak or laugh, as he fell onto the deck. His blood leaked from various wounds and onto the deck where it dripped in between the cracks.

We did it," Talicia said. "We won."

She dropped the sword and went to inspect Grimke's body.

I fell to my knees and looked from Colden, to Adonis, to Grimke, to Tanner, all laying unconscious on the deck.

"I wouldn't call this winning," I said.

Moments later, I passed out.

o

When I opened my eyes, I was lying in a field of lavender. The scent flooded my nostrils, and I leaned up on my arms. My body felt great, and I was relieved to not feel the aches and fatigue that I had expected.

"You're doing better than I could have hoped."

I looked toward the voice, but I knew who it was without seeing her. Sitting on a throne made of white marble inlaid with three large rubies at the top, I saw my mother, Moesha.

She looked exactly like the last time I'd seen her, but she appeared out of place on the weird throne and in those fancy clothes.

She was clothed in a long dress that faded from dark blue to light blue just below her waist. The dress was awfully long, and even though she was seated, it covered her feet. Bands of black decorated her waist and bodice, and the dress was sleeveless and revealed her arms. It was vastly different from the trousers and boots she used to wear when she planted lavender in front of our home.

Her kinky black hair was straightened and hung smoothly down her back.

"You're not dead," I said. "But this is just a dream, I guess."

My mother smiled.

"Yes, it is a dream, but dreams are where it's easiest to reach you."

There was a sound behind her on the other side of the wall and she turned, distracted for a moment.

"Look, I just wanted to say I'm proud of you. You're doing great. Go to Jemny, you'll be safer there," she said quickly. "You can't stay long."

"Wait, where are you? Where did you go? How could you leave us?" I asked, approaching her quickly.

"It was not my choice; it was for your safety. I had to go back home," she said, sadly.

She began to fade, so I ran towards her.

Just before I reached her, the door to the garden opened, and a small boy wandered in. I stopped and looked at him. He waddled over to my mother and climbed into her lap.

He had dark brown skin with long golden locks of hair. He smiled at the toy in his hands, not paying me any mind.

"What are you doing, Mommy?" he asked, looking up from the toy, but before my mother or I could speak again, she faded, and all I saw was blackness.

And then I opened my eyes.

The first thing I heard was the crash of the boat as it crashed into the shore. I bolted upwards and immediately felt the soreness in my body. I struggled to stand and saw Talicia at the helm, steering us.

She looked at me sheepishly and I smiled at her.

I considered telling her of our mother, but decided to wait and keep it to myself for now. *What was in Jemny? Why would we be safer there instead of here?*

I limped over to where Colden lay and placed my hand on his chest; there was no heartbeat. I cried over him silently and I could feel Talicia watching me.

I tried to compose myself, but my sorrow was swallowing me whole. I felt like Jesuit *had* thrown me overboard. I was drowning in the ocean and an unnamed monster had its tentacles latched onto me and was pulling me into the dark and icy depths.

I looked up and saw that we had crashed near the Eastern Aid Tower. This was where Jacob was left.

Colden would want to be buried with his father. I hoped the *Aegea* could still sail back to Pavrenes so I could bury them. I could even pick up some more Pavrenis while I was on the island. And if the boat couldn't sail anymore, perhaps I could rest and use the gurneys and make an aura bridge as Adonis had done.

I closed Colden's eyes and looked at his final smile. I fingered the bracelet he'd given me, then slid it onto my wrist, and latched it.

Ithil's light reflected off of the amethyst, giving it a ghostly glow in the dark.

I stood and went over to Grimke. He was breathing still to my relief, so I dragged his body up to the helm, careful not to tamper with his wrist.

Next, I checked Tanner and saw that besides a large knot on his forehead, he seemed all right. As I dragged him, he moaned Colden's name and I had to stop for a moment.

My breathing became ragged.

Talicia came over to help me, and together we dragged Tanner to where Grimke lay by the helm.

239

Lastly, we moved Adonis who was also alive. I was grateful he had saved Talicia and was in his debt. He had been saving us since we met him in Opulake.

How had he survived the lightning, yet Colden had died? Was it his dwarven blood or was it because the third bolt of lightning was smaller than the first two?

After they were safely put to the side, I went below deck with Talicia to check on the Pavrenis. Some had been rolled around from the impact, but none seem to be awake just yet. I wondered if it was because I'd given Grimke two plagicines instead of one, like everyone else in the sick house.

Once everyone was safe and readjusted, I went back onto the deck and stood there with Talicia. I looked north where I knew Jemny was. It would be a long journey to get there; it could take weeks if not months to finally make it. I wondered if it would just be us or if the other Pavrenis would follow us.

I knew Adonis would follow us to Fort Mudo at least, to meet up with Savant. It would be nice to see Arabella again, maybe I would try to reach out to her later once everyone woke up and some of my magic was restored.

I was exhausted but I had to remain awake, Talicia was the only other member of our party who was conscious.

I thought about my father and who he really was. At the end of the day, I was glad he was safe despite his lies. I wondered if I'd have issues with trusting him again, but it seemed he had cleared the air. Surely he couldn't be hiding anything else.

I glanced at Talicia, but she looked as good as she could after recent events. She was much stronger than I had thought. I was glad that she was my sister, and I cherished our bond.

The murder of Jesuit did not seem to bother her, but it weighed heavy on my mind. She coughed and smiled at me. I pulled Talicia close. I had lost Colden; I would not lose anyone else, no matter where our journey took us.

We would have obstacles, of course. The First Constellation still remained. The head of the snake had been cut yet sprouted another one in Olympia.

There also was Lord Cicero and the Green Lion Guild. They were from Cypress like my mother, and I wondered if they had done business together.

I wondered once again if Colden's mother was in Jemny.

Was my mother in Jemny? Who was the little boy in her lap? What would I say if I saw any of them?

It would be hard, but I knew no matter what I would find her. I would do whatever it took to find my mother.

I grabbed Talicia's hand tightly. We would find her together.

End of Book One

Trilogy Davis

Odessa and the First Constellation

Alphan II Index

Aid Towers: towers constructed during the reign of King Harlem that are spread throughout Damasyr and serve as an alert system across long distances, there once were eighteen but now only eleven remain

Alekisanit: the wielder of the sunfire sword *Sithos,* he was the first human to marry a dwarf

Alphan II: one of three planets that orbit the two stars Astria and Zaniah

Astria: the younger sun of Alphan II, it rises second and has a more orange hue

Banshees: different from spirits banshees are the leftovers of powerful magic and have a deafening shriek and are seen as omens of death in Damasyr

Callyssia: a luck seer from Cypress, she possessed the wish sword, Kurama, and was a great user of Djinni magic

Cypress: a jungle country to the southeast of Damasyr ruled by the Sea King

Damasyr: a kingdom formerly known as *Bruenor*, currently occupied by the second human kingdom

Djinni: magicians who bargain and serve as conduits spirits to gain elemental magical powers

Dwarves: the race that ruled Damasyr when it was called *Bruenor*, although they are not much shorter than humans, they were given their name from the giants who lived in *Bruenor* before them

Eloah: the god of the Elohan Faith

Giants: the race rose out of the ground two thousand years ago, although they did not name the land others called it *Gath*

Green Lion Guild: a dark guild in Cypress that oversees darker matters and are trained mercenaries

Humans: the main population of Damasyr during the fourth era

Inamorata: a magic bond made between lovers, it is the ultimate form of intimacy

Ithil: the purple moon that orbits the planet Alphan

Jemny: the royal capital of Damasyr ruled by the Queen

Kurama: a sword with a pommel shaped like a fox spirit and a blade that shimmers with red light

Luck Seers: those who use dice to tell fortunes, those who use dragon bones are the most accurate

Morale: a member of the Elohan religion who can manifest their Faith to a certain standard

Mystio: the first squad of the Damasyri military

Pigeons: used to deliver messages from settlement to settlement

Queenslen Forest: an allegedly haunted forest near Pavrenes on the unnamed island

Rangers: the third squad of the Damasyri military

Sunfire: enchanted fire used to make weapons with unique features, the practice has become rare

Sithos: a sword held by the Forever Prince Alekisanit; it was able to burst aflame when the secret magic word was spoken

The First Constellation: the largest bandit group in Damasyr, they have remained active despite attempts from the Queen to destroy their organization

Tripa: a title given to a temple head leader in the Elohan Faith, they report only to the Queen and the Most Elevated One

Tyvent: a country of islands to the east ruled by a council

Umbar: a slaver country southwest of Damasyr, the people here are said to conduct magic sacrifices in pyramids made of white marble, they coat their weapons in a venom that prevents wounds inflicted by the weapons from being healed with magic

Whey: a bread made with magic used to restore magic energy

Zaniah: the elder sun of Alphan II, it rises first and has a more yellow hue

Glossary

achuka- uh-choo-kuh

addemire- add-duh-mie-er

adonis- uh-don-is

aegea- uh-gee-uh

alekisanit- aye-el-kih-san-it

almonaster- al-mon-nast-stur

almonastian- al-mon-nast-stee-en

alphan- al-fan

analisa- an-nuh-lees-suh

arabella- air-ruh-bell-luh

arinia- a-ren-nee-uh

asia- ay-zhuh

astria- ass-stree-uh

augue- aw-gee

baluga- buh-loo-guh

barnabas- bar-nuh-bus

beidha- bead-duh

bentley- bent-lee

bjorn- byorn

bruenor- broo-nor

callyssia- cuh-liss-see-uh

chelsea- chel-see

cicero- sis-sir-ro

colden- coal-den

cypress- sie-press

damasyr- dam-muh-sear

damasyri- dam-muh-sear-ree

dedham- ded-ham

djinni- ji-nee

dresden- dres-den

drie- drie

drien- dree-en

eloah- ee-loe-uh

elohan- e-loe-un

elvira- el-veer-ruh

elyse- e-leese

estella- ee-stell-luh

estonia- ee-stone-nee-uh

eufaula- yu-fall-luh

felicita- fuh-liss-sit-tuh

fussiladi- foos-sih-lawd-dee

harlem- har-lem

ichor- ick-chor

ichorian- ick-chor-ree-an

inamorata- in-nuh-mor-rat-tuh

ithil- ith-thil

jackdaw- jak-daw

jacob- jay-kuhb

jemny- gem-nee

jemnan- gem-nen

jesuit- jess-su-it

joani- jown-nee

joel- jowl

judo- joo-doe

kurama- kuh-rah-muh

garcia- gar-see-uh

gath- gath

gianni- gee-on-nee

graham- gram

grimke- grim-key

Odessa and the First Constellation

laurens- lor-rens

ledonia- lee-doe-nee-uh

lito- lee-to

maia- mie-yuh

merica- mair-rik-kuh

micah- mie-cuh

mensae- men-sae

moesha- -moe-eesh-shuh

montoya- mon-toy-yuh

mudo- moo-doe

mystio- mist-see-oh

nori- nor-ree

numenor- noo-meh-nor

odessa- oh-dess-suh

opulake- opp-pew-lake

olympia- oh-limp-pee-uh

pavrenes- pav-rens

pavreni- pav-ren-nee

potiphar- pot-ti-fore

queenslen- kweens-len

ramona- ruh-mone-uh

rutabaga- roo-tuh-bay-guh

resyr- ree-sear

reyna- ray-nuh

roshni- rosh-nee

roe- roe

salia- sail-lee-uh

samson- sam-sun

savant- suh-vant

scout- scowt

sithos- sit-those

solace- soe-luss

sorbet- sore-bay

talicia- tuh-liss-see-uh

tamberli- tam-bur-lee

tawni- tah-nee

tanner- tan-ner

terza- ter-zuh

themyscira- them-mis-skere-ruh

tripa fons- trip-puh fons

tyvent- tie-vent

victoria- vic-tor-ree-uh

Odessa and the First Constellation

victorija- vic-tor-ree-uh

virginia- ver-gin-yuh

volo- voe-loe

whey- wae

ukiyo- u-kee-yoe

umbar- um-bar

zaebos- zie-bose

zaniah- zuh-nie-uh

About The Author

Trilogy Davis is a writer with over 10 years of experience. He is also a painter and content creator.

YouTube: Trilogy Davis

Website: trilogyeffect.net

He has written *Odessa and First Constellation*, *Arabella and the Tower of Magic*, *When Life Gives You Pineapples,* and is working on book three in The Legends of Damasyr series.

Other than writing and content creation, Trilogy loves reading, gaming, and going to new places.

www.ingramcontent.com/pod-product-compliance
Lightning Source LLC
Chambersburg PA
CBHW020315200626
46814CB00006BA/2254